A
Harlequin
Romance

1437

TO MY DEAR NIECE

by

HILDA NICKSON

HARLEQUIN   BOOKS
WINNIPEG   ●   CANADA

First published in 1970 by Mills & Boon Limited,
17-19 Foley Street, London W1A 1DR, England.

SBN 373-01437-6

© Hilda Nickson 1970

Harlequin Canadian edition published October, 1970
Harlequin U.S. edition published January, 1971

Printed in Canada

CHAPTER I

The letter from Aunt Maud arrived on one of those rare, still misty mornings in early summer which give promise of a fine, warm day. The dew was wet on the grass, the distant trees mysterious and aloof, the world silent, ethereal, and unspeakably beautiful.

Coming in from the garden for breakfast after an hour's weeding Vanessa picked up the letter from the hall mat. The name—Vanessa's own—and address was written in a thin, rambling scrawl and was barely decipherable, but Vanessa's father had been born in this house, and the postman brought into the world by her grandfather. Everyone for miles around knew the unconventional Dr Woodrow, and his pretty wife who sang the leading soprano roles in the local amateur operatic society.

Vanessa went through into the large kitchen where Hester, an elderly, distant relative who acted as general help and housekeeper, was setting the breakfast trays. No one had ever had breakfast in the same place. It was an eccentric household. Her father came of a family of eccentrics—or so they appeared to the more conventional. Great-Aunt Maud, who had never married, living virtually alone in a large old country house called Puck's Hill, its grounds for the most part overgrown with weeds because Aunt Maud would not allow chemical weed-killers to be used in case these poisoned the birds; Uncle Ted who owned a private zoo; a cousin living in a converted windmill in Norfolk on the edge of the marshes, her mother, hopeless at ordinary household skills, but an accomplished pianist and with the voice of an angel. One could go on. Even herself, filling the role of chauffeur/gardener at home. Not that she considered herself odd. It was a job she had drifted into, having no other immediate plans for a career. She had been educated at a boarding school, and it was typical of her father that when people asked what she was going to do ' when she left school ', he would answer:

' Do? Do? Why, she's just going to be herself. She's not being educated merely to earn money, she's being educated so that she can live a full and happy life.'

Vanessa could see now the sad smiles, the wise shakes of the heads. But fresh from the home of a friend whose parents had a beautiful garden to the wilderness which passed for the same thing at home, she had set about uprooting weeds, making flower beds, tending the stretch of grass which had once been a lawn in the days of old Joshua, her grandfather's gardener. Turning a wilderness into a thing of beauty had given her an immense amount of satisfaction. Then she began to drive her father on his rounds or out on emergency calls, and to run her mother to and from rehearsals and opera performances.

Life was good—or had been until her father had taken on a junior partner. Vanessa had fallen in love with the young doctor, but not he with her. Yesterday, he had married the equally young and very pretty district nurse. When they returned from their honeymoon they would be living far too near the Woodrows' house to make it easy for Vanessa to put him out of her thoughts. Not that anyone had ever known how she felt. She had kept it completely to herself—simple enough, surrounded as she was by people who were always busy or preoccupied.

She had her own breakfast in the big conservatory. Her mother would doubtless have hers in the bath; her father, with a book, in front of the French window of his study which overlooked the herb garden; and Hester, in the kitchen.

Half way through her breakfast Vanessa took out Aunt Maud's letter. Accustomed though she was to her great-aunt's scrawl, she still had difficulty in deciphering its contents, but two sentences stood out like banner headlines. *I have not been so well of late.* And: *I would dearly love to see you, child, if you could possibly come down for a few days.* Vanessa folded the letter thoughtfully, her features relaxing into soft lines. Dear, funny little Aunt Maud! She was sweet, but as tough and as independent as they come. Vanessa had been fond of her since childhood when she used to spend school holidays in the rambling old house full of passages and tiny rooms. Aunt Maud had devised treasure hunts in the untidy garden, built fairy and elfin houses, had taught Vanessa to appreciate nature, to learn about insects, birds, butterflies and all tiny creatures by seeking them out in their natural habitat, by sitting with quiet patience, watching and waiting. Waiting for them to appear and then watching what they did and how they lived.

Vanessa made a swift decision. She would go to Aunt Maud. Tomorrow. She would send a wire saying she was coming on the ten-thirty train. Another of her aunt's eccentricities was that she was not on the telephone, and it would be folly to trust the post. She finished her breakfast, then went outside again. She would tell her mother and father when she saw them. A family consultation about her decision was not necessary, neither would it be expected.

'Poor Aunt Maud,' was her father's comment when she told him as she drove him on his morning round. 'She must be ninety if she's a day. Go and see her by all means, my dear. Have you any money?'

'Not much.'

'Oh. Well, I'll make you a cheque out when we get back. You can cash it in the morning.'

'Thanks, Father. I hope you'll be able to manage.'

He smiled. 'I can't promise to weed the garden or spray the roses, but otherwise, we'll manage. Kenneth and Julie are due back at the end of the week anyhow.'

7

'Yes. Yes, I know.'

When she told her mother the news at lunchtime, her mother simply murmured absently: 'Yes, all right, dear. Give Aunt Maud my love.'

And so with fifty pounds in her pocket, Vanessa caught the ten-thirty train to Cringlewood, a small country town deep in the heart of Suffolk. Barnhill, the tiny village where her aunt lived, was some twenty miles from there. If the little branch line had been closed down, which was more than likely, she would have to get a taxi to take her the rest of her journey.

Puck's Hill, she mused. It was the name Aunt Maud had given to the house. She was rather puckish herself, Vanessa thought, with her wizened, weather-beaten features, her crinkly smile.

It took the train a little over two hours to reach Cringlewood, and as she expected, the branch line to Barnhill was now closed. Vanessa knew that buses ran only about twice a day, and these were unlikely to have been increased. She was going in search of a taxi when a girl about her own age with long dark hair approached her.

'Are you Vanessa Woodrow?'

'Yes,' Vanessa answered in a surprised voice. The girl was a complete stranger to her.

With a swift smile the girl held out her hand. 'My name's Freda Hamilton. Ian knew you were coming, so he asked me to meet you.'

'Ian?' Vanessa queried with a brief handshake.

'My brother. He was round at Puck's Hill yesterday when your telegram arrived.'

'You and your brother are friends of Aunt Maud?'

Freda Hamilton nodded. 'Ian especially. My car's just outside. Shall we go?'

Vanessa fell into step with the other girl. 'How is my aunt?' she asked, trying to remember whether she had ever met any friends of Aunt Maud.

8

'She's—not too good, I'm afraid,' was the answer. 'So we're glad someone has come. Actually, you're the only relative your aunt seems to talk about.'

Vanessa knew a twinge of conscience. Her mind had been so preoccupied in battling against her hopeless love affair, she had not written to Aunt Maud quite as often as usual.

'She does have other relatives, of course,' she told Freda, 'but not all of them understand Aunt Maud's funny little ways.' It was the kindest way she could put it. 'Anyway, she and I have always kept in touch, though I must admit I haven't written to her lately. I didn't know she was ill, naturally, otherwise—'

She broke off as they emerged from the station yard and her companion pointed to a green shooting brake.

'That's my car. It used to be Ian's, but he let me have it and bought another one.'

'How long have you and your brother lived in Barn-hill?' asked Vanessa as they drove out of the picturesque town with its narrow cobbled streets, half-timbered shops and houses and the colourful, straggling market.

'Not very long, I suppose, in terms of country life. About five years.'

'And you've known my aunt all that time? She never mentioned either you or your brother.'

'For the simple reason that we haven't really known her for very long. Your aunt has always been something of a recluse, hasn't she? Or so they say in the village, and we rarely saw her, either.'

It was true. Aunt Maud's home and garden had been her world, though at one time, the children of the village were always welcome in her wild garden. But as she had become older she had kept more and more to herself.

'How did you come to meet her, then?' she enquired.

'Ian went to see her one day. She asked him to stay to tea, and after that he was a frequent visitor.'

'And you?'

'Oh, I didn't visit her quite as often as Ian did. They —found things to discuss.'

Vanessa had detected a slight hesitation before the other girl answered, and was about to ask her what sort of things her brother had discussed with Aunt Maud, but Freda Hamilton went on:

'Ian and I wondered whether you'd care to come and have lunch at home with us. You'll find things a little disorganized at Puck's Hill.'

But Vanessa was anxious to see her aunt as soon as possible.

'That's very kind of you,' she answered, 'but if you don't mind I'd rather go straight to my aunt's. If things are as disorganized as you say, then it's high time someone did something about it.' Anxiety lent a sharp edge to her voice.

There was a pause, then the other girl said quietly: 'Yes, of course. I understand. I just thought it would give my brother a chance to—to meet you. But if you're staying for a few days—'

'I shall stay for as long as my aunt wants me.'

Though the other girl was very likeable and it was good to know that Aunt Maud had found someone to keep an eye on her, Vanessa could not help feeling slightly irritated. She frowned, trying to find out why. Was it really a guilty conscience about her own family, that their eccentricities caused them to be lacking in caring enough for each other, even for someone old like Aunt Maud? But then this applied also to her aunt. Each of them seemed to have one thing only, besides themselves, that they cared about. Her father had his medical practice, and he was a good doctor, but the rest of his time he lived in his own world. Her mother had her singing. Aunt Maud had her house and garden, but the world outside—apart from Vanessa herself—might not exist.

This Ian Hamilton. How was it that he had managed

to gain Aunt Maud's confidence sufficiently to become a regular visitor? Few people had, if any, so far as she knew. It was strange. Who was he? What had he and her aunt to talk about? His sister appeared greatly preoccupied with him—Ian this, Ian the other. He was obviously a person of some importance to her. It had been he who had asked her to meet Vanessa herself. Why? Why should he concern himself with her coming? Perhaps Aunt Maud had asked him to meet her and he had delegated the task to his sister.

Vanessa came to the conclusion that it was he, this man she had not even met, who was the cause of her irritation. She could almost hear him accusing her of neglecting her aunt. Well, she was here now, and there was no need for this Ian Hamilton to concern himself any longer.

She became aware that they had almost arrived. The car was now driving through the cool avenue of trees which formed part of the estate bordering on Aunt Maud's property. Vanessa suddenly realized that she had followed her aunt's lead in not taking much interest in the rest of the people who lived in the village. All she knew of the owners of this estate—largely woodland— was that it belonged to a wealthy landowner who used the woods with its house—aptly named The Lodge—as a country retreat, breeding pheasants for the sheer joy of killing them. He was known simply as the Colonel, though whether he had ever actually commanded a military unit was doubtful. But even this limited knowledge had been gained from snatches of conversation Vanessa had heard in the village shops. His name was never mentioned in Aunt Maud's house. A wicked man like that who bred God's creatures for the pleasure of killing them was beneath even her contempt. Vanessa caught a glimpse of a deer. Had the man added deer-shooting to his nefarious pastimes?

But the trees were thinning out, and a few minutes later Freda Hamilton turned her car through a wide gateway which led the way up a twisting drive to Aunt Maud's house. Vanessa was appalled at the neglect, the rank weeds, now eight or ten feet high, their thick stalks and umbrella-like leaves shooting up from the earth like nuclear monsters.

'Good heavens!' she breathed. 'I had no idea it was as bad as this. What's happened to Joe Simpkins who used to do the gardening?'

'He's still here. It's simply more than he can cope with. He keeps an area near the house clear, then tackles as much of the rest as he can. Your aunt won't allow—'

'I know. I'm not entirely in ignorance of my aunt's ways,' Vanessa felt stung to interpose.

'I'm sorry.' Freda Hamilton brought the car to a halt outside the front door of the old grey stone house with its porticoed entrance.

Vanessa sensed that she had given offence. She turned to the other girl.

'Do forgive me if I seem put out. I'm so worried about my aunt. I write to her regularly as a rule, but I'm afraid I've had problems lately and—'

Freda Hamilton gave a swift smile. 'Never mind, you're here now.'

Vanessa nodded. 'It was extremely good of you to meet me. Perhaps we shall see each other again.'

'I hope so,' the other girl responded.

They said goodbye, and as the car disappeared down the drive again Vanessa looked after it for a moment. A charming girl, even if she did seem rather under her brother's thumb. Where did they live, she wondered, and what did both she and her brother do?

The outer door of the house was flung back. Vanessa turned the knob of the vestibule door and stepped inside the wide hall which narrowed into a long passage with doors on either side. Immediately, a dusty, musty smell pervaded her nostrils. She wrinkled her nose and frowned. Dust lay thickly on the Jacobean oak furniture, the once colourful carpet was badly in need of cleaning. What had happened to Miss Gould, the companion-help Aunt Maud used to have?

Vanessa was about to climb the stairs when a door opened at the farther end of the long passage and Miss Gould herself appeared.

'Your aunt's expecting you, Miss Vanessa.'

Vanessa turned and went towards the woman, almost as small and frail-looking as Aunt Maud, and was struck at once by the tired look about her eyes.

'You look as though you could do with a rest, Miss Gould. How is my aunt?'

Miss Gould shook her head sadly. 'Not too good, miss. I wanted to get a nurse in, but she wouldn't hear of it. She just keeps drifting off, sometimes for a few minutes, sometimes for longer periods. At times she rambles, at others she's surprisingly lucid. She keeps asking for you, miss, and I'm glad you've come.'

'Is she in any pain? And has the doctor seen her?'

'Oh yes, he comes every day, sometimes twice. She doesn't seem to be in any pain. The doctor says it's her heart—and just old age. She's ninety-three, miss. But if only she would eat, I'm sure she'd gather a little more strength.'

'Is she asleep now?'

Nancy Gould nodded. 'I've only just this minute left her. Do you know what I think, Miss Vanessa?' Vanessa shook her head. 'I think your Aunt Maud's decided she's had enough of this world and has simply made up her mind to leave it.'

Vanessa felt her heart contract sharply. 'Oh, don't talk like that, please!'

'It's true, my dear. You know what she's like. Once she's made up her mind to a thing—'

'I know. But I hope you're wrong. I'll go up and see her. Would you like me to stay with her for a while?

You must have lots to do.'

Nancy Gould nodded. 'If you would, Miss Vanessa. I've hardly dared leave her side for weeks now.'

Vanessa's conscience smote her again. 'For weeks? But how long has she been ill? I received a letter written by her only yesterday. I could tell by her writing that something was wrong, but—' She broke off in distress. 'Oh, I do wish you had written to me, Miss Gould.'

'My dear, I wanted to. She kept saying you'd be writing in a day or two, then when the weeks passed and no letter came, she made me bring paper and pen and insisted on writing herself. If she hadn't mind you, I had quite made up my mind to drop you a line myself. If her condition had become really serious—urgent—I would have telephoned or sent you a wire. As it is, Dr Upson says she might go on like this for a year or more. He wanted her to have her bed brought downstairs, but she wouldn't hear of it.'

Vanessa sighed worriedly and went upstairs. She tapped softly on the green-painted door, but there was no response. She opened it quietly and closed it behind her, then walked on the balls of her feet towards the great double bed. At the foot she paused, and her heart as well as her conscience smote her. Dear, sweet, fragile Aunt Maud! She looked tinier and more puckish than ever, but weak and ill. Tears gathered in Vanessa's eyes, but suddenly her aunt's were wide open and looking straight at her.

'Hello, child. There's no need to tiptoe. I heard you arrive and I heard you come into the room. I have to pretend to be asleep sometimes, otherwise I'd never get any peace. Old Nancy hangs around me as if she were afraid I'd run away.'

Vanessa blinked and for a brief moment hovered between laughter and tears. She moved swiftly to the bed and dropped on her knees, putting her arms swiftly around the tiny figure.

'Oh, darling Aunt Maud! Why didn't you write to me before? I'll never forgive myself for—'

'Child, child—' The thin fingers clasped around Vanessa's hand. 'It's all right. I knew you'd come.'

Vanessa brushed her cheek against the velvet soft one of her aunt. 'I'd have come much sooner if I'd known you were ill.'

'Ill? Who says I'm ill? I never heard such nonsense. Stop fussing, child, and tell me what you thought of Ian Hamilton. One of these days I shall close my eyes and quietly slip away. But ill? Never.'

Vanessa brought up a chair and sat down. 'I—didn't meet him. His sister met me at the station and drove me here.'

'But didn't you have lunch with them?'

Vanessa shook her head. 'She did ask me, but I wanted to come straight home to you.'

'Tut, tut, child. But no matter. You will meet him soon.'

Her lids closed heavily. Vanessa eyed her aunt anxiously. Was she, in fact, slowly losing her hold on life, and not, as she had said, merely pretending to be asleep? Then suddenly the bright blue eyes were wide open again.

'Well? Don't look at me like that, child. You're getting to be as bad as Nancy. Go down and get yourself some lunch.'

'Very well, Aunt Maud, if you're sure you'll be all right. But what about your lunch? You must eat something.'

A thin hand waved her to be gone, and before Vanessa left the room the tired eyes were closed again.

Vanessa went downstairs thoughtfully. How ill was her aunt really, how close to the time when she would close her eyes for the last time? Tonight, if the doctor came, she would have a word with him. Meanwhile, she would help Nancy to get the house in some kind of order and look in on Aunt Maud from time to time.

After a scratch lunch Vanessa set about cleaning and polishing the hall, then went to the village shops while Nancy cleaned up the kitchen. She was making preparations for their evening meal when there was the sound of a car outside.

'That will probably be Dr Upson, Miss Vanessa,' Nancy said.

Vanessa whipped off her apron. 'I'll go and let him in. I want to have a word with him.'

She had never met the doctor and he looked younger than she expected, but he had that air of confidence and authority that most doctors have. His dark straight hair was parted at the side, his features were fine and clear-cut and his face tanned more like that of a man who lived an outdoor life—an interesting, rather than a strictly handsome face. His lean figure moved easily as he walked towards her carrying a basket of fruit.

He thrust the basket into her hands. 'For both you and your aunt. How is she?'

A little taken aback by his unceremonious greeting, she glanced at the delicious-looking peaches and grapes sitting on huge oranges and grapefruits.

'Well, I—was hoping you could tell me that.'

'Oh? I would have thought you could draw your own conclusions—aside from having a chat with the doctor.'

Vanessa was beginning to feel somewhat exasperated. 'I certainly do want to have a talk to you, doctor. Drawing one's own conclusions is not good enough with someone like my Aunt Maud. I want to know—'

She would have gone on, but the doctor's eyes widened, and the rather grave features relaxed into something like faint amusement.

'Did you call me doctor?'

She stared at him. 'Aren't you—'

'I'm afraid not. My name is Ian Hamilton.'

Vanessa drew an angry breath. 'It might have saved us both some embarrassment if you had introduced yourself, Mr Hamilton.'

His eyebrows shot up still further. 'I'm not embarrassed. You shouldn't jump so readily to conclusions. I've come to enquire about your aunt—and to see her, if she's—'

'My aunt is asleep. I don't think she should be disturbed,' she told him swiftly.

Ian Hamilton gave her a steady look. For a split second Vanessa felt something within her crumbling, then her lips came together firmly. He might have his sister under his thumb, and have somehow managed to gain Aunt Maud's regard, but he was not going to win her over so easily!

'I'll take your word for it,' he said, in a tone which clearly cast doubts on her truthfulness. 'But if your aunt asks for me at any time, I hope you will let me know.'

'Naturally. And now if you'll excuse me—'

She was appalled at her own rudeness. Why had she taken such a dislike to this man? It was quite unlike her.

A noticeably steely look came into Ian Hamilton's grey eyes. Then he turned and went back to his car without another word.

As his car crunched its way down the drive, Vanessa sighed heavily and went indoors again. She couldn't think what had come over her. She had not even thanked him properly for the fruit.

She took the basket upstairs and quietly opened the door of Aunt Maud's room, hoping that she was indeed sleeping. But the blue eyes were wide open.

'I heard a car,' she said at once. 'Who was it?'

Vanessa noted mentally that her aunt missed absolutely nothing.

'It was Ian Hamilton,' she was forced to answer.

'He brought you this basket of fruit. Isn't it lovely?'

'Ian?' demanded Aunt Maud. 'Why in heaven's name didn't he come up?'

'I—thought you were asleep.'

Aunt Maud eyed her fiercely. 'So you prevented him from coming up to see me? Why?'

Vanessa shook her head swiftly, thinking she had better humour her aunt.

'No particular reason. I've told you, darling, I thought—'

'You didn't come up to find out whether I was asleep or not, did you?'

Vanessa did not know what to say. This cross-questioning was quite unlike her aunt. But she was saved from having to make any reply by Aunt Maud speaking again.

'What did you think of him?' she quizzed

This, too, was difficult. 'Well, I—only spoke to him for a few minutes.'

'Mm! You didn't like him, did you? That's easy to see. But no matter. He and I exchanged a few sharp words the first time we met, I remember. Take the fruit downstairs, child, and eat it yourself. I hope you thanked him nicely.'

Once more Vanessa was saved from answering an awkward question. This time by Aunt Maud closing her eyes.

Dr Upson arrived a short time later. Vanessa talked to him while Nancy was persuading Aunt Maud to eat a little dinner. He confirmed Vanessa's fears that her aunt was having periods of unconsciousness rather than merely pretending to be asleep as she said.

'Your aunt has had a good innings,' he told her. 'She has led a very active life, as you may know, even if she has kept to herself. She's kept this huge place clean with very little help as well as doing a great deal of the gardening.'

'Yes, I know. So you—don't think she'll ever get up again?'

He shook his head. 'No, I do not, Miss Woodrow, though how long that obstinate heart of hers will continue to tick over, I can't tell you. Will you be staying with her long?'

'As long as she needs me,' she assured him.

Vanessa wrote to her parents saying that she would be staying with Aunt Maud for an indefinite period. She helped Nancy to spring clean the entire house and took turns in sleeping in the dressing room attached to her aunt's bedroom, in case she wanted anything during the night. It soon became evident that day and night were one to Aunt Maud, and that dreams and reality, past and present, were merged into one in her confused mind.

Repeatedly, she spoke to Vanessa by name. Once, she murmured—and Vanessa did not know whether she was awake or asleep,

'Vanessa, don't ever sell Puck's Hill. Promise me.'

'Darling, of course I won't.'

Vaguely, she wondered whether her aunt had made out a will, or if not, who was her nearest relative. Vanessa's father? But she put aside any serious thought of her aunt's passing. It was too unhappy to contemplate.

She was in one of the village shops one morning and the proprietor asked how Aunt Maud was and made one or two comments on her life. The other customer in the shop was a young man whom Vanessa had never seen before, but as new houses were being built in the village all the time, this wasn't surprising.

When she went out, however, the young man followed her. 'Can I give you a lift back to Puck's Hill, Miss Woodrow?' he asked.

She looked at him in surprise. 'How do you know my name?'

He grinned disarmingly. 'Didn't I hear Mrs Green call you by it just now? Anyway, the whole village has heard about the charming niece of Miss Woodrow of Puck's Hill who has come to stay.'

Her lips curved in amusement. 'Flattery goes right over my head, Mr—'

'Kendal's the name. Miles Kendal—but please don't call me Mister.'

He was very likeable, she decided. 'In that case, my name is Vanessa,' she told him. 'But we're not likely to meet very often. I'm helping Miss Gould to look after my aunt, and when she's—better, I shall be going back home.'

'That would be a pity when we've just got to know each other—your going home, I mean,' he added hastily.

Vanessa smiled and said she must be getting back to Puck's Hill, but Miles Kendal said persuasively:

'Look, why not come into the Swan and have a sherry with me or something? I can't say have a coffee because as you know we don't sport a café in the village. I met your aunt once, and I thought she was a wonderful woman.'

At this, Vanessa found her resistance weakening. 'You've met my aunt? How?' she queried.

He took her arm. 'Come and have a drink and I'll tell you. I know you must be wanting to get back, but if you let me drive you, you'll be there quicker than you would have been if you hadn't met me and had to walk.'

Vanessa laughed. 'All right, you win.'

The Swan was a homely sort of place with its oak beams, low ceilings and interesting examples of copper ware. They sat in the little parlour, whose floors and furniture gleamed with years of polish.

'How *is* your aunt, really?' Miles Kendal asked gravely when they were seated and served. 'Do you honestly think she *will* get better? They say she's getting on for a hundred.'

Vanessa shook her head sadly. 'Everyone's life has to come to an end some time, I suppose. But I'd rather not talk about it.'

He smiled. 'I understand, and I think it's wonderful that you've come all this way to look after her. She must mean a lot to you—and you to her, I imagine.'

'We are fairly close, I suppose.' She went on to tell him how she used to spend her holidays with Aunt Maud and the sort of games they used to invent. Miles Kendal listened with close interest.

'You're not her only niece, are you?' he asked.

'Oh no, but my father is her only nephew.'

'Her next of kin, in other words.'

Vanessa frowned, hating the expression now that her aunt was nearing the end of her life span.

'Why do you say that?' she asked, an edge to her voice.

'I'm sorry,' he said swiftly. 'It's just that—I felt I wanted to warn you, as it were.'

'Warn me?' she echoed.

He smiled faintly. 'I didn't mean to sound dramatic, and I realize you don't want to dwell on things, but the fact is, your aunt has a sizeable bit of property there, and some people, with no sense of rightness or delicacy of feeling are already hovering around her like —well, like vultures, wanting to buy the place.'

Something inside Vanessa contracted sharply. 'Who do you mean exactly?'

He shrugged, as if unwilling to mention anyone's name. Then he said: 'Well, I expect you'll meet him sooner or later, if you haven't already. I mean Ian Hamilton. He's already made your aunt an offer.'

Vanessa drew a swift breath. 'So that's it!'

Miles Kendal nodded. 'That's it. I take it you and he *have* met?'

'We certainly have. But Aunt Maud will never sell. I'm sure of it.'

'Maybe he's hoping she'll change her mind.'

'Then he doesn't know my aunt. She'll never change her mind, and—' She broke off, unwilling to repeat her aunt's injunction never to sell. 'But as a matter of interest, why does he want to buy such a big place? Has he a family?'

'If you mean has he any family of his own, he isn't even married. He and his sister live together in that place called The Lodge. But I expect you know that.'

Vanessa shook her head. 'No, I didn't.'

'No? Well, of course, his place is more or less a playground. Or should I say a sportsground. You must have heard of the Colonel.'

'I have—to some tune.'

The news that Ian Hamilton was now the owner of those acres of private woodland in which defenceless birds were hunted made her dislike him more than ever.

'His little hunter's paradise adjoins your aunt's place, as you may know,' Miles Kendal went on. 'The man is just land-hungry. And what he'd do with Puck's Hill if he got it, heaven knows. Pull it down, I expect.'

'Not if I can help it,' muttered Vanessa determinedly. She rose to her feet. 'If you don't mind, I really must be going.'

'Don't look now,' Miles said as they left the Swan and went towards his car, 'but there's Hamilton and his sister now in that expensive-looking car across the road.'

'I don't want to look,' she said angrily. 'And I wish to goodness he'd keep away from Puck's Hill.' How the man had managed to win her aunt's confidence, she didn't know, but she vowed he would never win hers.

She would have pretended not to see them, but to her surprise Miles Kendal gave them a wave and a smile and called out: 'Hi, Ian!'

Vanessa found herself almost forced to look their way. After all, Freda had been kind enough to meet her at the station. And so she gave a slight wave, being careful to look at Freda only. She could not help noticing, however, that there was no answering wave for Miles Kendal from Ian Hamilton. He looked decidedly put out. Miles chuckled as if something were amusing him, and put his hand under Vanessa's elbow to help her into his car.

'Do you know Ian Hamilton very well?' she asked him.

Miles shrugged. 'Well, you know how it is. One has to keep on something like friendly terms with people, even if one doesn't agree with what they do or how they live.'

Vanessa did not agree with him. 'I shall never make any pretence of liking him.'

Miles started the car and cast an amused smile at her. 'As bad as that?'

'Why should one pretend? I think I disliked him before I even met him. I know that sounds terrible, but it was the way his sister kept talking about him, as if his word was law. Then he came to see my aunt and let me go on thinking that he was the doctor, and— oh, I don't know—'

'*I* do. You find him generally irritating. He gets me that way too, so you're not alone. I think it's that superior manner of his. But I'm rather surprised you don't like him—in a way—because most of the women hereabouts, including his sister, are absolutely gone on him.'

'Really? Perhaps that's what's wrong with him. He expects every woman to come running, and if they don't it doesn't please him. It's made him conceited.'

'I'm glad you're not taken in by him, anyway,' answered Miles Kendal, turning into the driveway of Puck's Hill.

Characteristically, Vanessa began to feel guilty about her attitude towards Ian Hamilton. She shouldn't have spoken like that about him to someone else, even though she did dislike him. After all, there must be *something* likeable about him for Aunt Maud to have such a high regard for him.

Miles Kendal was eyeing the rank weed growth flanking the drive.

'Heavens! I wouldn't like to be the person who takes on this little lot. Couldn't you persuade your aunt to do something about it?'

'She won't have chemical weed-killers used,' Vanessa answered. 'And in any case, I wouldn't dream of bothering her about it while she's ill.'

'No, of course not,' he murmured, in a conciliatory tone. He brought the car to a halt outside the front door of the house and got out to open the door of the passenger side for her. When she thanked him, he said: 'It would be nice to see you again. May I?'

She hesitated. 'I'd like to, of course, but I'm afraid I can't make any arrangements while Aunt Maud is so ill. I might see you in the village some time when I'm shopping, but in any case I'm not here permanently, so—'

He put his hand into an inside pocket. 'Tell you what. Let's say same time and place next week. If you can't make it, don't worry—maybe you will the week after, and if there's ever anything I can do any time, here's my address.' He gave her a card.

She glanced at it briefly, then thanked him and they said goodbye.

But exactly one week later, Aunt Maud passed peacefully away in her sleep. Vanessa telephoned the doctor at the kiosk a short distance from the house, and with him, within five minutes, came Ian Hamilton. Vanessa was too shaken with grief to resent him, and in the days preceding the funeral, she was grateful to him for the way he took charge of everything, and to his sister for all her help. After the interment she turned to thank them both, Ian in particular, feeling rather ashamed of the opinion she had formed of him.

' I don't suppose we shall ever meet again,' she told him. ' I shall be going back home as soon as I've helped Nancy put the house to rights. But I would like you to know how grateful I am for all you've done. I hardly know how to thank both you and Freda.'

Freda murmured: ' Only too glad to have been of help.'

But Ian said stiffly: ' I shouldn't bother to try. Anything I did was for your aunt's sake.'

Vanessa felt decidedly snubbed. Even Freda gave her brother a swift glance of protest. To hide her feelings, Vanessa moved on to speak to one of her aunts.

Actually, few of Aunt Maud's relatives had come to the funeral, though Vanessa had notified all those whose whereabouts were known to her. Vanessa's mother had stayed away, saying she detested funerals, and though her father had motored down, he had already left again. Vanessa wished they would all go—Ian and Freda included, though during the past week she had grown to like Freda very much indeed.

But soon all had left, leaving Nancy and Vanessa alone again.

The day after the funeral Vanessa caught the train into Cringlewood. Aunt Maud's solicitor had asked to see her. Vanessa could not think why, as it was most unlikely that her aunt had any money to leave, and the house would surely be left either to Nancy Gould or Vanessa's father. She hoped, to the former, as Nancy was more in need than her father. But Aunt Maud was just as likely to leave it to the National Trust or a wild life preservation society. Perhaps she herself was a trustee or something like that.

The solicitor, a bright and surprisingly young man, began by offering his sympathy to Vanessa on the death of her aunt.

'She was a very interesting and unusual woman.'

'Eccentric,' Vanessa supplied with a slight smile.

'Yes, I suppose you would say that, and like all eccentrics she left a rather unusual will. You will not be surprised, I'm sure, to know that she left a considerable sum of money to a local bird sanctuary, also to her friend and companion, Miss Nancy Gould. To her relatives she left absolutely nothing—with one exception —yourself. Even so, there are conditions attached.'

'Conditions? What sort of conditions?'

But the solicitor shook his head. 'That I am not allowed to tell you. It's to be held in trust for six months, after which time, my fellow trustee and I will decide whether or not you are entitled to it.'

Vanessa couldn't help smiling. 'Aunt Maud always did like playing games. But I didn't know she had any money.'

'Oh yes. It's a very considerable amount. Your aunt accumulated it for the simple reason that she never spent any—or very little.'

'And if I don't fulfil the conditions?' Vanessa queried.

'Then the money all goes to the bird sanctuary. But there's something else.'

'Yes?'

'Your aunt has left the house and the entire estate to you—unconditionally.'

CHAPTER II

'To me?' Vanessa echoed. She could scarcely believe it. 'But—but why me?'

The man behind the desk smiled. 'You're too modest. I would have thought it was obvious. She left the thing she valued most to the person for whom she had the highest regard.'

But Vanessa shook her head in denial. 'You're very kind, Mr Oliver, but I'm sure it would have been more appropriate if Aunt Maud had left the house and land to Miss Gould. What on earth am I going to do with a house that size?'

'I'm quite sure your aunt knew what she was doing, Miss Woodrow. You'll do the right thing with it, I've no doubt of that, and there's no need to worry about Miss Gould. Your aunt has left her well provided for.'

Vanessa felt too bewildered for the time being to think straight. Mr Oliver rose and held out his hand.

'You'll soon get used to the idea. And if you have any problems, I'll be glad to advise you in any way I can.'

She shook hands with him and thanked him. Then as she reached the door, he added:

'By the way, Ian Hamilton was a very great friend of your aunt. I'm sure he will be happy to give you any help or advice you need too.'

Vanessa smiled politely and made her way down the spiral of stone steps, vaguely trying to assess how she felt about Ian Hamilton—and why, and at the same time hazarding a guess as to his opinion of herself. But her thoughts either way did not progress very far. As she stepped out on to the pavement she almost collided with Ian.

'Good morning,' he said, not looking in the least surprised to see her. He glanced upwards to the solicitor's office window. 'I see you've paid your visit to Mr Oliver.'

'Why, yes. Do you know him?'

'Of course. Your aunt mentioned to me that he was her solicitor. Have you—heard some good news?' he queried.

'I—I think so.'

'What do you mean—you think so?' he demanded.

She fought down a swift reaction to his interrogation. 'I mean I'm not sure yet. I haven't had time to think about it. A large house like that—all those grounds. It's a terrific responsibility.'

'That's so.' He glanced at a nearby clock. 'Look, it's almost on lunch time. Would you come and have lunch with me and maybe talk about it?'

She hesitated, then almost, it seemed, against her will, she thanked him, and he put his hand under her arm and marched her off down the street. She was beginning to get a glimmering of what made Ian Hamilton tick for some people—the strong, forceful personality of the man. That and more. Much more.

He led her through a doorway sandwiched between a hardware store and a gardening shop, then up a flight of stairs.

'This is the place to come to if you should ever be in town and wanting a meal,' he said. 'It's quiet, unpretentious, the food's good—and it's licensed. I don't think much of any place if you can't have a glass of wine with a meal if you want it. It's called the White Horse.'

Now he was telling her where she should eat, she thought. His taste might not be the same as hers in the least, though he seemed to take it for granted that it would be.

But when they reached the top of the stairs and he led her into the restaurant she was agreeably surprised. The place was beautifully and very tastefully decorated

28

with clever lighting, flowers on every table and a deep pile carpet on the floor in rich wine colour. It was evident that he came here often from the way he was greeted by name by the head waiter and by the girl who served their meal.

'You like it?' he asked, as her gaze flitted from one point of the decor to another.

She nodded. 'It's very nice. But whether I shall come here very frequently, if at all, depends on their prices. I have very little money, I'm afraid, and unless I get a job of some kind—' She broke off. 'I'm sorry. I was speaking my thoughts aloud. I hadn't meant to trouble you—or anyone—with my problems.'

'That's all right,' he said quietly. 'Perhaps you wouldn't mind telling me what the news was from your aunt's solicitor. I take it from the little you said earlier that she has bequeathed to you her house and land.'

'That's so.' She told him the rest. 'I don't know what the conditions are with regard to the money in trust, but I don't really want my aunt's money, and—'

His eyes opened wide. 'You can't really mean that.'

She gave him an angry look. 'Of course I mean it. The only thing is, I don't know how on earth I'm going to keep the place up. Even if I do get a job, what I earn will only keep me, it won't pay for anything to be done on the house or—'

'Or what?' he prompted.

'Or even heat the place adequately in winter.'

'You certainly have a problem. Do I take it that you intend living at Puck's Hill?'

'Of course. What else? I'm sure that's what Aunt Maud would have wished.'

'I expect so. I thought you might consider selling the place. As you say, it's a large house, certainly too big for either one or two, supposing Miss Gould stayed on with you.'

Vanessa frowned. Into her mind with startling clarity

29

came the things Miles Kendal had told her—that Ian Hamilton wanted to buy Puck's Hill, that he had already made her aunt an offer and that he was land-hungry.

'I shall *never* sell Puck's Hill,' she flung out emphatically. 'Not to anyone.'

Ian Hamilton inclined his head and gave her a calculating look.

'That's how you feel at the moment, I'm sure, but it might be a different story in a few months' time. However—' he went on swiftly, as an angry denial sprang to Vanessa's lips—'I take it you're going to take up residence and do the best you can for the house and property. What sort of a job do you do?'

Vanessa drew a deep breath. 'I work for my parents —or did. My father is a doctor, as you probably know, and I act as his secretary, do the gardening and drive the family car.'

A hint of a smile curved at Ian Hamilton's mouth. 'It sounds as though you'll be very well equipped to look after Puck's Hill. But won't your father miss you?'

'He will understand. And he won't miss me so much as he might have done some months ago. He—has a new partner now who—who has just married, so—'

'I see. You talked of getting a job around here, but somehow I don't think you'll find it necessary.'

She gave him a puzzled look. 'What do you mean?'

'Oh, you'll think of something,' he said evasively, and as if to assist him the waitress came with their second course.

So much for the 'help and advice' Mr Oliver said Ian Hamilton would be happy to give, Vanessa could not help thinking wryly to herself. All he was interested in, seemingly, was the future of Puck's Hill. Well, she had promised her aunt she would never sell and she would keep that promise. But how was she going to live without getting a job, and if she was out at work all day how was she going to be able to look after the place?

'Don't look so worried,' Ian Hamilton told her. 'You'll make out, I'm sure of it.'

If Vanessa had not been so puzzled by this and his other rather ineffectual remark she would have been irritated. But somehow she couldn't help feeling that such banalities from him were out of character.

'I shall have to do some hard thinking, anyway,' she answered.

He gave her a steady look. 'Well, when you come up with some conclusions I'll be interested to hear them,' he said, much more characteristically, Vanessa thought fleetingly. Then he went on: 'Meanwhile, as you're in town why not take the rest of the day off and I'll show you round?'

Vanessa hesitated. She felt sure he would be the most uncomfortable person to be with. On the other hand, there was no bus back to Barn Hill until four-thirty.

'We could include a look round some of the shops,' Ian Hamilton added disarmingly.

Vanessa could not resist a smile. 'You make it difficult for me to say no. But I would like to get home about five-thirty. Nancy will be expecting me back by that time, and I wouldn't like her to worry about me. As you probably know, we're not on the phone.'

He nodded. 'I'll get you back all right, but you should think seriously of getting on the phone. I tried to persuade your aunt, but she said she'd managed all these years without one and would continue to do so.'

Vanessa's eyes gleamed. 'No one could ever persuade Aunt Maud to do anything she didn't want to do.'

Ian Hamilton eyed her keenly. 'And what about you? Are you just as obstinate?'

'I can be—yes,' she told him, 'if obstinate is the term you would use for someone who knows their own mind and won't allow themselves to be manœuvred

31

first this way, then that.'

He made no comment, but Vanessa could guess what he was thinking and was glad. She did not know whether she was considered to be obstinate or not, but she had certainly been brought up to make her own decisions, and once having felt a course of action was right, to stick to it and not allow herself to be talked out of it. She hoped he realized that no power on earth would persuade her to sell Puck's Hill.

She knew Cringlewood a little, but that was all. Ian showed her the more interesting buildings in the old part of the town, the merchant's house dating back to the fifteenth century, now a museum and art gallery; the Elizabethan Theatre, recently restored; an old coach-house inn; a narrow cobbled street with its pink and whitewashed houses and shops which sold and displayed all the old crafts and artists' materials, and finally the ancient market square, still in use with its wonderful floral and plant displays.

Now they were on foot, and presumably on a sudden impulse, Ian bought a bouquet of sweet-smelling freesias and thrust them into her hands.

'In memory of Aunt Maud,' he said as if he was afraid she might misconstrue the gift.

'Thank you,' she said. 'I'll put them on her—'

'No, don't,' he cut in sharply. 'She wouldn't like that at all. Put them in your room or at any rate somewhere in the house.'

He was an odd sort of person, she concluded. Difficult to know, difficult to understand, difficult also, she surmised, to please.

'Well, now for the shops,' he announced. 'We have only three large stores, but they sell pretty nearly everything between them, and all have a top floor tea room.'

Each of the places had some very beautiful things—china, glasswear, furniture, fabrics and, naturally, clothes. Afraid of boring him, she was careful not to wander too long among the many dresses, coats, suits and hats, but Ian obviously sensed this.

' Go on,' he urged. ' Don't mind me. Take all the time you want.'

But some of the clothes were so fabulous, so smart and so desirable, and Vanessa had so little money it was really rather depressing to linger. She sighed at the recollection of her meagre wardrobe and turned away.

' A cup of tea would suit me better at the moment— and time is getting on.'

' This way, then,' he said briskly.

During tea she suggested that she should catch the bus home, but he wouldn't hear of it.

' I'm your neighbour,' he said. ' Remember?'

She was not likely to forget. But she had been in danger of forgetting how poor defenceless creatures were hunted down on his land and shot. How *could* Aunt Maud have liked him? she wondered again.

' What's on your mind?' asked the object of her thoughts.

She gave a slight start. What a disconcerting man he could be! There was not a flicker of the eyebrows or a look or gesture which he missed. But she was not to be led into disclosing what she had been thinking.

' It's on my mind that I ought to be getting home— if you don't mind,' she answered.

' All right.'

He rose immediately, much to her inner annoyance. She had not expected him to take her up quite so quickly, and had intended finishing her cup of tea. But now she had no option but to follow his lead.

He spoke very little as he drove through the Suffolk countryside. From time to time Vanessa stole a glance at his stern profile and the uncompromising mouth and jaw. A man to be reckoned with, she thought. He was a good, competent driver, courteous to other road users, calm and unruffled in the face of some blatant bad driving, and Vanessa found herself watching his strong hands on the wheel in a sort of strange fascination. She was so entranced she hardly even noticed when they drove through his woodlands. Afterwards she was annoyed with herself. She had meant to ask him one or two questions about himself and his property— whether he had been related to the Colonel, whether he had bought the land or had it bequeathed to him, and just exactly what he did—besides hunting. But he deposited her at the front door of Puck's Hill and made off, giving her barely enough time in which to thank him.

Vanessa had two visitors that evening, Miles Kendal and Freda Hamilton. Miles was the first to lift the great, old-fashioned front door knocker.

'I would have called sooner,' he said, 'to offer my sympathies on your aunt's death, but I didn't want to intrude on a private and family affair.'

'That's all right. But it's nice to see you.' She invited him in.

'I've been thinking about you,' he said as he stepped inside. 'In spite of your aunt being so ill her death must have been a great blow to you. I know how fond you were of her.'

Vanessa led him into the small sitting room, a favourite of Aunt Maud's which she used instead of the large drawing room, because it overlooked a quiet part of the garden. Here, she could open the French window and put out food for the birds and the squirrels and sit and watch them. This was one area of the garden at any rate which was relatively free from the rank weeds which choked the rest of the grounds. Aunt Maud dug them up herself but still retained all the wild flowers which other people called weeds.

'Yes,' Vanessa said in answer to Miles. 'It was a wrench, but Aunt Maud's personality was so strong it almost seems as though she's still here.'

Miles frowned slightly. 'It will be like that for a

while until you get over it.'

Vanessa gave him a glance of faint surprise, but she made no effort to contradict him. Aunt Maud had set her seal so firmly on this house and garden, her influence would always be felt.

'What—will you do now?' Miles asked after a short silence. 'Will you be staying on here or—has your aunt left the place to someone else?'

Vanessa smiled. 'No, she's left it to me—and I'm glad. At first I think I was a little overwhelmed at the thought of owning all this—the responsibility and so on. But now I'm glad. I don't think I would have liked anyone else to have it. They might have been tempted to sell it or something.'

Miles eyed her uncertainly. 'You mean—you're glad because of the affection you had for your aunt?'

'Of course. What else?'

He was still puzzled. 'Do I—er—take it your aunt left you a sufficiently large sum of money to pay for its upkeep?'

Vanessa laughed shortly. 'No, as of this moment she hasn't.'

'Good lord! Then what on earth are you going to do?'

'I don't know yet,' she told him cheerfully. 'I haven't had time to think.' It was useless telling him of the sum of money left in trust for her, she thought. She might never get it, not knowing the conditions under which she would be entitled to it.

Miles looked at her curiously. 'But it's terrible, really, leaving you this great house with the grounds in such an appalling condition and no money to do anything about it. Just think of the heating too, in the winter.'

'Winter is at least six months away,' Vanessa told him. 'Now I've recovered from the first shock, I regard it in the nature of a challenge.'

Miles shook his head. 'That's all very well, Vanessa, but you've got to be practical.'

'I will be,' she assured him. 'But let me offer you a cup of coffee.'

He thanked her and followed her into the big, old-fashioned kitchen.

'You're not alone in the house, are you?' he queried as he watched her make the preparations.

She told him about Nancy. 'She's probably in her room. If she comes down I'll introduce you.'

'Is she staying on with you?'

She nodded. 'Aunt Maud left her a legacy. We talked things over earlier this evening after I'd come back from seeing the solicitor, and she wants to stay on as before and make this her home. In return for a couple of rooms, she'll support herself and help with the work of the house. An ideal arrangement.'

Miles shook his head. 'You mean your aunt has actually left a sum of money to her—and not to you, her own "flesh and blood" as they say? It sounds monstrous to me.'

'It isn't at all,' Vanessa answered. 'In fact it would have been appropriate if my aunt had left Puck's Hill to *her* instead of to me.'

Miles Kendal gave her a long look. 'You know, Vanessa, you're an extremely generous person. In fact, you're quite a girl. The only thing I'm afraid of is some people taking advantage of your good nature.'

'Such as—whom?' she queried.

'Well, Ian Hamilton. I wouldn't mind betting he's already made some kind of approach about your selling Puck's Hill.'

She laughed briefly. 'He has, as a matter of fact. I ran into him outside the solicitor's office.'

'What?' Miles Kendal gave a sound of derision. 'I knew it. And don't tell me that your running into him was accidental. It's my guess he knew you'd be seeing the solicitor this morning and was hanging about outside waiting for you to come out. He probably asked you out to lunch, I shouldn't wonder.'

Vanessa's eyes widened. ' I must say you're making some very accurate guesses. He didn't look very surprised to see me, and he did take me out to lunch, as a matter of fact. But don't worry about Puck's Hill. I shall never sell it—and I told Ian Hamilton so.' She picked up the coffee tray and Miles followed her back to the other room.

' I'm glad you made it plain to him, anyway. But tell me, was it laid down in the will that you mustn't?' he asked.

She was interrupted by a knock at the front door, so excused herself and went to answer it, to find it was Freda.

' I came to say how pleased I am that you're staying on at Puck's Hill,' she said.

' That's kind of you. Come on in. You're just in time for a cup of coffee.'

Vanessa led her into the small sitting room. ' You two do know each other, don't you?' she asked.

Freda looked very surprised to see Miles there. They both nodded, and Miles looked oddly amused.

' Miles came to offer his condolences,' Vanessa explained to Freda. ' I suppose your brother told you my news?'

' Yes, he did. But if I'd known you had someone with you, I'd have come another time.'

' Don't mind me,' Miles said. ' I shall be pushing off pretty soon, anyway.'

There was a rather strained silence and Vanessa sensed that the other two had no great liking for each other.

After a while, Freda turned to Vanessa. ' I suppose it's too soon for you to have any ideas as to what you're going to do with the place?'

Miles sipped his coffee. ' Maybe she's just going to

live in it. I forgot to ask, Vanessa—and I'm sure you won't mind. Have you by any chance a private income of your own?'

She shook her head. 'Enough to live on for about another week, that's all.'

'Stone the crows!' he said expressively.

'If I'm any judge,' Freda said, 'Vanessa won't be content just to " live in it ".'

'But what else, for heaven's sake? You're not suggesting she should take in lodgers?'

Vanessa laughed. 'Maybe I'll start a fruit farm or something.'

'First get rid of the weed,' Miles told her, '—And that'll cost a fortune in chemical weed-killer.'

Vanessa frowned and made no reply. Even if she could afford a chemical weed-killer she couldn't possibly use one when her aunt was so much against them. She didn't know what the answer was at the present moment, but she did not want to start a discussion—possibly an argument—with Miles. Freda, she noticed, was saying nothing on the subject. But Miles Kendal was looking at Vanessa questioningly, so she had to answer him.

'Maybe I'll team up with Joe Simpkins in digging them out by hand,' she said with a laugh. 'After all, " if seven maids with seven mops "—' she quoted.

'Yes, and that's just about the size of it,' Miles said emphatically. 'Like seven maids with seven mops trying to sweep the sea shore free of sand. I tell you, Vanessa, without money you've got a pretty near impossible task here.'

'Have some more coffee, Miles,' was Vanessa's answer.

But Miles shook his head. 'I must be going, but I hope you'll let me come again.'

'Of course.'

Vanessa excused herself to Freda and showed Miles out. 'Thanks for dropping in. It was nice of you,' she said sincerely.

He grinned. 'Pity we were interrupted.' Then he paused for a moment before he went on: 'I—er—should watch out for Freda, if I were you. She's a nice enough girl, but—well, she does tend to echo her brother. She'll probably act as his—sort of emissary.'

'With what object?' she asked quietly.

'Well, you know. He wants this place. Oh, neither of them will ask you right out, but they'll try to con you in various ways, you'll see.'

But Vanessa couldn't accept that entirely. She felt sure Freda was trying genuinely to be friendly. She gave a light-hearted laugh.

'Well, thanks for the warning, anyway.'

'When can I see you again?' he asked, his hand on the door handle of his car.

'I don't know. I think I'm going to be pretty busy. Just drop in when you're passing.'

'Thanks, I will—and maybe we can go for a run some time or have an evening out in town.'

'That would be nice—but I'd better go now because of Freda.'

Freda had stepped outside into the garden. 'Sorry to have kept you waiting,' Vanessa said.

'That's all right. I only hope I didn't intrude too much.'

'Of course not.'

But Freda obviously had something on her mind. 'Do

'What makes you say that?' she asked.

Vanessa shrugged. 'Well enough. Why do you ask?'

Freda frowned. 'I should be wary of him if I were you.'

Vanessa almost laughed aloud—two people each using almost the same words to warn her off the other! you like Miles Kendal?' she asked.

'Didn't you know? He's a property developer. He's hoping to buy Puck's Hill at a giveaway price.'

Vanessa could no longer hide her feeling of amusement.

'What's the joke?' asked Freda.

'Well, *he* says that Ian wants to buy it, that he's already made my aunt an offer.'

Freda drew an angry breath. 'Yes, he has, but only because—' Then she broke off. 'I'm sorry. It's really none of my business. Ian would be furious if he knew I'd so much as mentioned it. Let's talk about something else, shall we?'

'As you like.'

So Miles Kendal and Ian Hamilton were business rivals, concluded Vanessa. Both wanted to buy Puck's Hill. For a moment she did not know whether she was amused or angry or hurt. Neither had been really honest with her, Miles least of all.

'What on earth will you *do* with all this weed?' Freda was saying, a note of despair in her voice as she glanced around the grounds.

Vanessa shook her head and looked at it, growing from the earth like monster rhubarb with its thick, fleshy stalks, the huge umbrella-like leaves, more and more fronds uncurling both at the base and up the stalk. Wild rhubarb she used to call it as a child.

'Dig it up, I suppose, little by little,' she answered.

Freda shook her head. 'Really, Vanessa, you're as bad as your Aunt Maud!'

'Maybe,' Vanessa answered laconically.

Freda glanced at her swiftly. 'Vanessa, I'm sorry. I didn't mean—'

'That's all right, I know you were only joking,' Vanessa told her. 'All the same, I do have a loyalty to Aunt Maud. I wouldn't like to do anything she'd disapprove of. I shall just have to feel my way. After all, there *are* parts of the garden free of this stuff. I don't know whether chemical weed-killers harm the birds or not, but in any case I couldn't afford to use them.'

'No, I suppose not,' murmured Freda.

Conversation flagged after that. Vanessa wanted to be alone to think things out, to make plans, and Freda seemed ill at ease, so Vanessa was not sorry when she departed.

Nancy was in the kitchen washing up the coffee cups. 'You shouldn't have done those,' Vanessa told her. 'I don't want you waiting on me.'

Nancy smiled. 'I'm not waiting on you, am I? Only washing up.'

Vanessa picked up a cloth to dry them. 'We've got to have a talk, Nancy, you and I—make plans.'

'I thought we'd had our talk, Miss Vanessa. Any other plans you make will suit me.'

'Well, to begin with, you must stop calling me "Miss". You're not my servant. Just call me Vanessa.'

'All right, if that's what you want. But if I were you, I wouldn't try to make too many plans tonight. Leave it until morning.'

'But I can't stop various things from running around in my mind. What I was thinking was, if you're going to pay your way here as you want to, then you must have Aunt Maud's little sitting room for yourself. The thing is, would you find the housework too much on your own?'

'Good heavens, no, Miss—I mean, Vanessa. I know the place was in a pretty bad state when you arrived, but then I had your Aunt Maud to look after. She wasn't very demanding, but I used to spend quite a bit of time in her room. Why do you ask? You're not going away, I hope?'

Vanessa shook her head. 'It's just that I shall probably be spending a good deal of my time out of doors. I must do something to start earning some money.'

'Such as?' queried Nancy with a sidelong glance. 'I

hope you're not going to go back on what we said earlier this evening. If I'm going to carry on as before and do the housekeeping, I can surely buy food for the two of us. Your aunt left me enough money to keep both you and me put together for the rest of our lives.'

Vanessa gave her a grateful hug and said no more, but she could not go on living on Nancy's legacy indefinitely.

While it was still light Vanessa had a good walk around the garden area and the rest of the grounds. There was the large barn which had possibilities. Its only purpose at the moment, apart from housing a few garden tools, was to provide a nesting place for the many swallows which came regularly every year. In the past Aunt Maud had sometimes given parties in it for the children of the village. Vanessa stood and regarded the place. It was big enough to hire for village dances—bingo, too, whether or not one approved of such a futile pastime. It was worth considering.

Quite close to the barn was a large greenhouse and she was reminded of the one at home, bright with pot plants. Perhaps she could make money by raising plants from seeds and selling them. But she had no money with which to buy glass for the many broken windows, and in the winter she would have to buy fuel for the heating. It was all very difficult.

What *had* Aunt Maud expected her to do with Puck's Hill except just live in it? It was only with the greatest difficulty that Vanessa ploughed a way through the weeds which choked the grounds beyond the small area of garden. On one side, separating the grounds from the road which ran through the village was a high wall, along the surface of which grew Virginia creeper, ivy and other evergreens. At intervals there were trees Great oaks, chestnuts, sycamores and a large number of common beech. On the opposite side there was a wide ditch and a hawthorn hedge, and at the lower end which bordered on Ian Hamilton's land was a straggling line of Scots pines—self-seeded from the Colonel's woods.

Vanessa went as near the boundary as she could, half expecting to see Ian Hamilton himself strolling beneath the trees with a gun in his hand, the typical squire who idled his time 'huntin', fishin' and all that'. Dusk was falling now, however, and she could not see very well, but it looked as though considerable clearing was being done. She wondered why.

When she went indoors again Vanessa wrote to Hester asking her to pack her clothes and other personal belongings and send them to her, and also to her parents telling them about Aunt Maud's bequest and her decision to make Puck's Hill her home.

She came to the conclusion that the only thing she could do which was not going to cost money, was to work outside, so the following morning after tidying her room she went in search of Aunt Maud's gardener, Joe Simpkins. She found him about to start mowing the small lawn at the back of the house. He was a man of about forty and looked tough enough for anything. She said good morning to him and told him that she was now the owner of Puck's Hill and would be living here.

'I take it you're willing to stay on?' she asked him. Nancy had offered to pay his wages for the time being.

'Certainly I am,' he told her. 'I've worked for your aunt ever since I was sixteen, an' it suits me fine. I've got my own bit of garden where I grow my vegetables and so forth, and my wife does three days a week at the Lodge, so we manage fine.'

She explained to him briefly the necessity of earning money in some way.

'I haven't made any definite plans yet,' she told him, 'except perhaps to let the barn for various purposes, but the first problem is to get rid of some of this weed. Maybe you'll help me to clean out the barn one day when it's too wet to work in the garden.'

43

But at the mention of the weed, Joe had started slowly shaking his head.

'You'll never get rid of all that stuff without weed-killer, miss. I've been trying for years, but it's futile. Your aunt—'

'Yes, yes, I know—the birds. But in any case the cost of chemical weed-killers would run into hundreds of pounds—and I just haven't got hundreds of pounds. So together, you and I will just get digging—if you don't mind.'

'I don't mind. I'm used to it and while I'm doing one job I can't go doing another. But what about you, miss? It's much too heavy work for you. The roots of these things go deep.'

'I'm used to hard work, too. You are speaking to a fellow gardener, Mr Simpkins. I've been doing little else for the past two years. So I'm afraid the lawn and the flower beds will have to be neglected for a little while until we can maybe afford more help.'

He shrugged. 'Just as you say, Miss Woodrow, but don't call me Mister. My name's Joe.'

'Right, Joe.'

He produced a spare spade, but she found uprooting the obstinate weed to be hard and tiring work. Warm work too, as the sun was now blazing down, and after about an hour and a half Vanessa felt as though her back was breaking. She was thinking longingly of a cup of coffee and a short rest when she heard Nancy call out, and when she turned she saw Ian Hamilton standing there watching her.

'You look busy,' he said unnecessarily.

She felt in the pocket of her jeans for a handkerchief with which to wipe the perspiration from her face, but couldn't find one. Up to now she had simply used the back of her hand. With what seemed to her like a cynical smile Ian Hamilton took one from his pocket and handed it to her.

'Clean this morning. Unused.'

She hesitated momentarily, then as she felt a trickle of moisture begin to run down her nose, she thanked him and mopped her face.

Nancy was setting out a small wicker table and two garden chairs under the shade of a sycamore.

'Coffee's ready, Miss Vanessa!' she called out.

'Thank you, Nancy.' She noticed that the older woman had called her Miss once more. By force of habit or because of Ian Hamilton's presence? But for whatever reason Vanessa said nothing for the moment. 'Would you care for a cup of coffee?' she asked Ian Hamilton politely.

'Thanks. That would be very nice.'

She had half expected him to decline and wondered why he had called. But she led the way to where the chairs and the table were set out and sat down thankfully.

Ian Hamilton regarded her in speculative silence for a moment or two, then he remarked:

'You're doing a very noble job of work there.'

She sighed. 'I don't see anything "noble" about it. It's a first essential.'

Vaguely, she knew she was deliberately misunderstanding him. She had the feeling he had been trying to be complimentary, but somehow she simply could not stop herself from feeling faintly antagonistic towards him. She was wondering why, when Nancy came out with the coffee—all set out on a tray for Ian's benefit, Vanessa did not doubt. She and Nancy did not usually bother with such formalities.

'You've only brought two cups, Nancy,' she said, glancing at the tray. 'Mr Hamilton is joining us.'

'The other cup *is* for Mr Hamilton, Miss Vanessa. I'm having mine indoors and Joe will have his in his usual place.'

'Nancy—' Vanessa began in an admonishing tone. But Nancy affected not to hear and called out to Joe to

45

come to the kitchen for his coffee.

Vanessa suppressed a sigh. 'Black or white, Mr Hamilton?'

'White—but strong,' he answered, 'and two good spoonfuls of sugar.'

Evidently he expected her to sugar it for him. 'Is that to your liking?' she asked, a hint of sarcasm in her voice, as she offered him a cup of dark brown coffee, particles of demerara sugar dissolving on the surface.

'Looks fine,' he answered.

She offered him a biscuit, but he declined. 'I'll have a smoke, if you've no objection.'

He pulled out a pipe. *I might have known it,* she thought. He didn't look the type at all who would smoke cigarettes. She poured her own coffee and sweetened it while he filled his pipe. He paused in the act of striking a match.

'I'm sorry I haven't a cigarette to offer you.'

'I don't smoke, thanks.'

He struck his match and drew on the smooth brown pipe. 'Have you made any plans yet or thought any more about getting a job?' he asked.

He sounded almost schoolmasterish, she thought, or as if he were her guardian or something. She tried to remember that as a friend of Aunt Maud he had a certain interest in her.

'I don't think I shall go out looking for a job, anyway,' she told him. 'There seems to be more than enough to do here—'

'If it's only digging out weeds, eh?'

'Well, it's a job which in my opinion *has* to be done,' she answered sharply.

He gave her a swift, sidelong glance. 'But not necessarily by the sweat of your brow, surely?'

'How else? Chemical weed-killers are out of the question.'

'On what grounds?'

'If you were a friend of my aunt you must know how she felt about weed-killers.'

He took out his pipe and looked at it thoughtfully for a moment.

'Yes, I do know. But I'd like to know how *you* feel. I know how costly a job it would be to clear this little lot by sodium chlorate or something like that, but suppose you had the money, what then?'

Vanessa frowned and thought for a moment. 'I still wouldn't,' she decided suddenly.

'Why not? Because of your aunt's influence?'

'Not entirely, though she taught me more than any other person to appreciate wild life of all kinds, and if there *is* any possibility that chemical weed-killers would poison the birds and other small creatures, then—'

'Well, some say they do, some say they don't, but it's going to be the only way you'll get rid of all this quickly and without a lot of back-breaking work.'

'I'm not afraid of work,' she told him with determination. 'Naturally, if I had the money I'd employ extra labour. In the meantime, while the weather is good, I shall carry on digging up the weed.'

'And when the weather is bad?' he prompted.

But she felt she had answered enough of his queries. 'You're asking a lot of questions, aren't you, Mr Hamilton?'

'I'm interested,' he answered smoothly. 'And by the way, the name is Ian.'

It was on the tip of her tongue to retort that she did not feel like calling him Ian, but checked herself. Why was she so tempted to be rude to this man? She counted ten and answered his query, ignoring for the time being the reference to his first name.

'When the weather is wet, I might get Joe to help me tidy up the barn.'

'With what object? To let it for barn dances or something?'

47

She gave him a surprised look. 'Something like that. How on earth did you guess?'

'It wasn't difficult. You mean that's what you *are* thinking of doing?'

She nodded. 'It wouldn't bring in very much money, I know, but then, it wouldn't cost anything to clean up either. And it would be a start. I'd let it to anyone who wants to hire it, either for dancing, bingo, political meetings or anything.'

'Not a bad idea, but of course there *is* the village hall, you know.'

'Thanks for the encouragement!'

It was out before she could stop it, but Ian Hamilton did not seem the least bit put out.

'Just reminding you, that's all. Any other ideas?'

'I thought I might make use of the greenhouse. I'm —fairly good with plants. I could grow some flowering pot plants to sell for Christmas and next spring.'

'Ah now, that *is* a good notion. Long term—or at least, fairly—of course, but the idea does have possibilities.'

'The only trouble is, quite a number of panes of glass are missing.'

'That's no problem,' he said promptly. 'I'll get one of my men to come and fix those for you.'

'It isn't the fixing I'm worried about,' she answered. 'It's the cost of the glass.'

'That's no problem, either. I've got plenty of glass lying around at my place,' he said in a voice which brooked no argument.

But Vanessa did not want to be indebted to him. 'I'd rather pay my way—thanks all the same.'

He did not give away his feelings by so much as the flicker of an eyelid, but he rose and knocked out his pipe.

'All right. I'll send you a bill and you can pay me when your plants begin to pay. Thanks for the coffee.

I'll leave you to get on with your digging.'

His tone implied that he thought her efforts rather futile. He strode off down the weed-flanked drive and Vanessa gazed after him for a moment or two angrily. Then all at once she found herself admiring the way he walked, his firm yet loose-limbed strides, the way he swung his arms and held his head. But this was ridiculous! She picked up the tray quickly and took it into the kitchen.

In spite of a rest at lunchtime Vanessa ached in every limb by evening. How on earth was she going to stick this day after day? she thought despairingly.

Fortunately for Vanessa's aching back—though in the light of a new day, she told herself she would get used to it—it was pouring with rain the following morning. Joe said he could manage the clearing out of the barn himself, so Vanessa took a good look into all the rooms of the house, beginning with the attic packed with the usual kind of bits and pieces. At this juncture Vanessa made no attempt to start sorting it out. That was a task which would take weeks. There was a various assortment of chairs with torn upholstery and protruding springs, an old sofa of the chaise-longue kind, an ancient cabinet gramophone with no innards and trunks and empty cardboard boxes by the dozen, also faded pictures and piles of stuff which at the moment were unidentifiable or piled one on top of another.

As she went from room to room, some of them unfurnished, others filled also with what could only be described as junk, Vanessa toyed with all kinds of ideas. Some rooms were large, others quite small. One could have the house converted into a number of flats. But that would cost money, and not only did the idea not appeal to her but she felt sure Aunt Maud would not have approved. A guest house? But what attractions were there at Barn Hill apart from those of a pleasant country village? She could not think of anything which would not cost a great deal of money.

She wandered into her aunt's room where there were drawers and cupboards which ought to be looked into and cleared out. Clothes and other personal effects could not just be left to rot. In the drawers of the dressing table was an assortment of underclothes of the old-fashioned kind. What Nancy did not want could go to a village jumble sale. In the top drawer were various trinkets and ribbons. Nothing of any great monetary value, but Vanessa would keep them for memory's sake. The cupboard which passed for a wardrobe was almost empty. Two coats, one light-weight, one heavy, two winter dresses and a summery one which Vanessa remembered quite well. Poor dear Aunt Maud! She had spent very little either on herself or on the house. On the floor of the cupboard were two pairs of shoes and one or two empty boxes. Vanessa was about to shut the door again when she caught sight of an old-fashioned hat box tied with a piece of string. She picked it up thinking it might contain old letters or other souvenirs.

She untied the string and flung back the lid, then almost dropped the box. In it were rolls of pound notes, and on top of them was a letter addressed to herself.

CHAPTER III

Vanessa stared at the contents of the box for a moment unable to believe her eyes. Then she carried it over to the bed and took out the letter and read it.

Vanessa child, here is a little money to tide you over for a few months until you find your feet. I know you've no money of your own. Bless you and keep you. Your Aunt Maud.

Vanessa felt tears prick her eyes. Dear, sweet little Aunt Maud! What sacrifices of personal comfort she must have made to have saved this. The money was in bundles of fifty and there were half a dozen altogether. If all the bundles contained the same number of notes, there would be three hundred pounds. Not a fortune, but enough for her to live on until she began to earn money, enough to pay for the repair of the greenhouse, employ extra labour for weed clearance, to buy plant pots and potting soil, to heat the greenhouse when the weather grew colder, to pay a year's rates or anything else urgent which cropped up.

At the bottom of the box were old letters, some of which were from Vanessa herself, others tied with black ribbon-velvet were apparently love letters from someone called John. Why had Aunt Maud never married? Perhaps the letters would reveal the answer, but Vanessa felt it would be trespassing on her aunt's privacy to read them. For the time being she put them back in the box and went to find Nancy to tell her what she had found.

Nancy was not in the least surprised. ' I had a feeling she would do something like that. She was certainly what some people would call odd in many ways, but somewhere hidden away she had a shrewd, practical streak. I've often seen her with that old hat box, but I would never pry into things that didn't concern me, and

51

your aunt knew that.'

' But where did the money come from?'

' I can only guess, Miss Vanessa. You know, at one time your aunt owned a lot of property in the village. Cottages, plots of land and so on. She'd go out and collect the rents and never bother to put the money in the bank. And in later years she got into a habit of selling things. Jewellery, pictures, things of that nature. It started when we had one or two burglaries in the district. She said she wasn't going to have her bits and pieces stolen. As I said to her, they could steal money just as easily and that was a lot more difficult to trace than articles. But she wouldn't listen. She said she'd put the money where no thief would dream of looking for it. She was always afraid the house might one day catch fire, too. She said she could easily pick up her money, whereas she might not have time to go running round the house for various things.'

Vanessa smiled. ' It sounds just like Aunt Maud. But what happened to her cottages and other property? The solicitor didn't say anything about them.'

' She sold those too, Miss Vanessa, and a rare old profit she made in some cases. Plots of land, for instance, for building purposes. You know how values have risen. As the older folk who rented her cottages died, she sold those at a handsome profit too. Cottages she hadn't paid more than a hundred for fetched a couple of thousand or so.'

Vanessa smiled ruefully. ' And I thought she was poor —apart from this old house.'

' That was another of her notions. It was what she wanted people to think.'

If the house had been on the telephone Vanessa would have rung Ian Hamilton and told him not to bother about sending his man to glaze the greenhouse windows. She could now afford to have it done by a glazier.

Excited at the prospect of starting on her pot plant

project, she put on a raincoat after lunch and went into the village to see what flower seeds could be bought. But the shops who did sell seeds—the general store and the little chemists—had a limited variety. There was a preponderance of vegetable seeds, wallflower seeds and annuals, but no cinerarias or other of the greenhouse plants she had had in mind, such as the popular winter cherry, browalia or exacum. With the vague idea of perhaps being able to raise and sell wallflower plants if she could clear a space outside, she bought several packets of these seeds.

An idea occurred to her as she walked back to the house. An idea which became a strong conviction. That was the use to which she ought to put Aunt Maud's land. For growing things. For growing plants which would bring colour and beauty to the world, not those ugly weeds which choked everything else. She would grow tall spires of lupins, and delphiniums, scarlet and yellow geums, bright golden coreopsis and sunflowers, as well as all the wonderful half-hardy annuals which many people had not the time, space or heating to grow. Asters and petunias in their glorious array of colours, sweet pea plants, exotic zinnias, sweet scabious, gloriosa daisies and many more. A thousand and one things. Vanessa's imagination ran riot as she almost skipped back to Puck's Hill.

'All that, Miss Vanessa, on four packets of seeds?' Nancy quizzed jokingly when Vanessa told her excitedly about her plans.

Vanessa laughed. 'Yes, I know. It sounds crazy, doesn't it? But I'm going to make Aunt Maud's garden into a real show place, you'll see.'

'And how long do you reckon that will take you?' came a masculine voice behind them.

They swung round. Ian Hamilton stood in the open doorway of the kitchen, wearing a raincoat and a country cap, his pipe in his mouth, but unlit.

Vanessa recovered herself swiftly. 'I don't know how long it will take, but whether it takes six months or six years, I shall do it.'

He pursed his lips and inclined his head. 'Well, as a step in the right direction I've come to find out how many panes of glass you need for your greenhouse.'

Her chin went up. 'That's very kind of you, Mr Hamilton, but I have the money to pay for that to be done now.'

'Oh, really?'

'Yes, I've discovered a little—nest-egg, as it were, left for me by my aunt.'

'Ah, I thought it wasn't like her to leave you entirely without resources. But I take it it's not an over-large sum?'

She told him the amount, while behind her she heard Nancy putting on the kettle for tea.

Ian Hamilton heard the sound too. 'I always come at the right time, don't I? A cuppa would be just fine.'

Vanessa had to stop herself from retorting that he should wait to be invited. Nobody seemed to realize that this was *her* house. But of course, Nancy had been living here for so long.

'Yes, well—' Ian Hamilton said, examining his pipe in his usual fashion, 'I wouldn't be too ready to turn down offers of help, if I were you. Your money will melt quite soon enough, you'll find. My man will be here in the morning and if it makes you feel any happier you can pay him for his time.'

'I want to pay for the glass too,' she insisted.

He regarded her in silence for a moment, then said reasonably: 'It's been hanging about my place since goodness knows when. I'm only too glad to get rid of it. It was in danger of getting broken.'

She did not know what to say to that. The natural, normal thing, of course, would be simply to thank him, but with Ian Hamilton she was anything but normal and seemed to have a natural antagonism. Evidently taking her silence for consent, he turned to go. But at the same moment came the sound of the teapot lid dropping on to the teapot.

Vanessa roused herself to be polite. 'Will you stay for a cup of tea, Mr Hamilton?'

She fully expected him to refuse, as her attitude was anything but friendly, she realized that. She was still calling him Mr instead of by his first name, and even asking him formally to have tea could be taken as a hint that he ought to wait to be invited. But Ian Hamilton appeared impervious to all these considerations.

'Thanks,' he said.

She led the way into the library—one of the rooms she had not yet had time to attend to. But it had two comfortable chairs, a floor to ceiling window with a pleasant aspect and seemed more suitable in which to have tea at the moment than the larger drawing room.

Ian Hamilton looked round the room with interest, his glance ranging up and along the rows of dusty-looking books, most of their titles all but obscured with age and use, and to the large Adams-style fireplace.

'It's rather a fine old house, this,' he remarked. 'I haven't been in this room before.'

Nancy brought in the tea, then went out again. 'I haven't used it very much myself up to now,' Vanessa answered. 'And I can't remember Aunt Maud using it much either. I'm not sure yet what to do with it.'

'How do you mean?' he asked.

Vanessa frowned a little. He had a habit of asking questions to which she had not even thought out answers for herself.

'Well, I don't believe in having rooms that are not used, nor books which are never read, for that matter. I must get around to having a look at these—find out what they are and whether they're worth keeping.'

He took the cup of tea she offered. 'You're very practical. Tell me, how far *will* your aunt's wishes count with you? You don't seem to me the kind of person who will allow sentiment to influence your decisions.'

Vanessa thought for a moment. 'I don't know that there's a very clear-cut answer to that one. I'm sure my aunt would expect me to have a mind of my own.'

'I'm glad to hear you say that, and I think you're right.'

'Do you?' she came back swiftly. 'Why?'

He took a sip of his tea before answering smoothly: 'Well, I'm quite sure your aunt—from what I came to know of her—would never want to bind you to anything or impose any restrictions on you. At least, not as far as the house and what you do with it is concerned. She has left it to you without any conditions, hasn't she—I presume?'

'That's right,' Vanessa answered stonily. 'If I wanted to, I daresay I could sell the house tomorrow.'

Her words seemed to electrify him. He shot a sharp, piercing glance at her.

'I thought you said you'd never sell,' he said accusingly.

'So I did, but circumstances might lead me to change my mind, mightn't they?'

She was not serious. She had no intention of ever breaking her promise to Aunt Maud, and she was not quite sure what was making her say these things, except out of some inexplicable desire to provoke him.

His mouth hardened and he put down his cup and rose to his feet.

'Well, if you do happen to change your mind, perhaps you'd be good enough to let me know, or at any rate to put it on the open market and not let any Tom, Dick or Harry of a property developer have first chance.'

' I would choose carefully, I promise you,' she told him.

' Thanks for the tea,' he said stiffly. ' If you'll excuse me I must be going.'

He strode out without waiting for her to see him out. Vanessa sighed and stood with her arms crossed, each hand gripping the other arm tightly. What on earth was the matter with her? What had made her goad him in that way? Why pretend she might sell when she had no intention of doing so? She had not even entertained the idea that one day she might be forced to, if she could not earn enough money to keep the place up.

Then she told herself it was the way he had talked, telling her how practical she was, that she wasn't the kind of person to allow sentiment to influence her decisions, that her aunt would never want to bind her to anything. What had he meant by ' anything'? Had he guessed that Aunt Maud had extracted a promise from her? She had found out one thing anyway. He still wanted to buy the house.

But although she justified herself, she went about for the rest of the day feeling very ragged and at odds with life.

After tea she began looking at the books in the library. It had occurred to her that she could use this room as her office or study. But it would need redecorating before she could feel really happy in it, and she was not sure that she liked these floor-to-ceiling bookshelves. The stern, heavily-bound volumes towered above her intimidatingly. She would prefer low bookshelves containing bright, friendly-looking books backed by pale walls and perhaps wall lighting.

The books on the lower shelves were mainly classics— Dickens, Shakespeare, Thackeray, Walter Scott. These would rub shoulders quite happily with the books of more modern authors. There were a great many books on birds. These too she would keep. Those on the top shelves for which she had to climb on a step-ladder were frowning, dusty volumes of the history of the Crimea, the Boer War, the Great War. All very interesting, no doubt, if one had the time to plough through them, but Vanessa felt sure there were collectors of such books who could put them to far better use than she ever would. There was little point in letting them remain forever where they were gathering dust.

She was glancing once more along the shelf containing the books on natural history and birds when she came across a book on plants. She reached for it eagerly and flicked over the pages, walking over to the window. Then all at once her attention was riveted by a drawing. It was of a plant called the *Heracleum mantegazzianum* or Giant Hogweed.

It was the weed Aunt Maud had in her garden.

Vanessa turned over the page to find the script. *The largest umbelliferous plant in the world. Habitat, Caucasus.* She read on. It was a biennial, so took two years to reach maturity. It grew from ten to fifteen feet high—that was Aunt Maud's weed all right. Its sap could cause a rash on some people, sometimes taking the form of blisters. Involuntarily Vanessa looked at her hands. But fortunately she was in the habit of wearing gloves for heavy gardening work. Naturally, the book gave no hints of how to get rid of the weed.

Vanessa sat back in the chair and tried to think. Like most weeds, it flowered, seeded and propagated itself by the seeds falling when they were ripe. If one dealt with the weeds before they flowered, this served to control them. But if one simply cut off the heads they would go on producing more flowers and seeds in an effort to propagate themselves. But cutting off the seed or flower heads could act as a sort of first aid measure. Yes, that was the first thing. None of these weeds must be allowed to flower and seed. Those which were not seeding would be first year plants which would flower next year. They were the ones which should be uprooted this year. Approached this way, the solution to the problem sounded simple. Joe, of course, had not identified the weed, few people would, as it was not very common, and Aunt Maud had not bothered her head about it. Killing even an obnoxious weed was not in her nature. Vanessa remembered she would never even have flowers in the house because it was 'unkind' to cut them or break them off. But in Vanessa's view these weeds were choking the very existence out of other plants and flowers. Like the bullies and dictators of life they would take over completely if nobody had the courage to fight them.

By sundown the rain had cleared and the following morning, the air was dry and warm. Vanessa was explaining to Joe her discovery about the giant hogweed when to her surprise Freda drove up in her shooting brake accompanied by Ian and two other men. The men immediately got out and began unloading squares of glass from the back. Freda lowered her window.

'Lovely morning, isn't it?'

Vanessa went towards them. 'Hello, there! Nice to see you.' Feeling guilty on account of her rudeness to Ian the previous evening, her gaze slid past Freda to include him in a smile. 'I've been finding out things about this weed,' she told him.

Ian inclined his head. 'Such as?'

'Won't you come in and have a coffee, both of you, and I'll show you where I found it,' she said, still feeling penitent.

Freda and Ian exchanged a glance. 'We haven't come to take up your valuable time,' Freda said. 'And we've just had breakfast, as I suppose you have. Actually, we thought you could use some extra help, but we don't want to intrude, if you'd rather not have us around.'

Vanessa's conscience smote her harder than ever.

'Oh, Freda, how can you say such a thing? I'm always pleased to see you. But as for using extra help, I can't keep trespassing on your good natures.'

Freda grinned. 'Say no more! Just tell us what you want us to do. Come on, Ian.'

She got out of the car and Ian did the same. 'What have you been finding out about this weed, then?' he asked.

She told him, but as she was quite unable to remember the Latin name for it, still less pronounce it, she brought the book from the library and showed them the illustration and text.

'That's it all right,' Ian pronounced. 'And from what it says about the sap you'd better wear gloves when you handle it.'

'I've brought some anyway,' Freda said. 'You and the men haven't, though, have you?'

'Well, neither they nor I need actually handle it,' said Ian. 'If we do the digging, you girls can pick it up and stack it ready for burning, that would be the best thing.' Vanessa simply could not help the thought going through her mind that he was like a foreman giving orders, but she did not want to say anything to offend him when he and Freda were being so helpful.

Ian was watching her face. 'What's the matter? Have you got some other ideas?'

'I have, as a matter of fact,' she answered. 'I'd thought it a good idea to go around with some shears and cut the flowering or seeding heads off before they ripen and fall. That will at least save new plants from springing up next year.'

'All right,' Ian said as if giving his permission. 'But watch out for that sap. And start at the far end of the grounds away from where the men and myself are working. For one thing there's no point in cutting off the heads of those we'll be digging up, and for another, the sappy ends will probably dry out if left for another day.'

He dropped the book on to the low table and strode out purposefully.

'By the way,' Freda said as she and Vanessa followed him, 'congratulations on finding the little nest-egg your Aunt Maud left for you. I imagine it will make all the difference.'

Vanessa admitted that it would. 'At least I shall be sure of being able to pay the rates and electricity bills for a year or so.'

'And maybe get on the phone?' suggested Freda.

'Perhaps,' agreed Vanessa.

In less than no time at all Ian and one of the men, along with Joe were digging away at the weeds while Ian's other man set about putting panes of glass in the greenhouse. Armed with a pair of shears and a short-handled scythe Freda and Vanessa began slicing off the flowering and seeding heads.

'Ian and I were wondering whether you'd like to join a club that we're members of,' Freda said as they worked. 'We meet once a month and have the occasional party.'

'What sort of club?' queried Vanessa.

'It's a Foresters'. There's a fair amount of forestry in the area, as you know, and Ian is by way of being a forester, so—'

'Is he?' asked Vanessa curiously.

'Why, yes, didn't you know?'

'How should I? I did notice the other evening that some clearance had been done on your side of the fence, but it was getting dark.'

'You must come and have have a meal with us and see around the place. Why not make it Sunday lunch? You've got to take a little break some time,' she added, seeing Vanessa's hesitation.

'Yes, I—suppose so. It's just that I'm anxious to get the greenhouse into production. But perhaps we can talk later.'

She moved in the opposite direction to Freda. It occurred to her as she grasped the tops of the hogweed and slashed at them before dropping them on the ground, that it would save time and a second handling if she and Freda dropped them into boxes or cartons as they went along, then filled the wheelbarrow and took them to a central place for burning afterwards. So she went into the house and brought some of the cartons Aunt Maud had hoarded in the attic.

When she went outside again she glanced over to where the men were working and involuntarily she stood and stared.

Rather surprisingly, following yesterday's rain, the sun was hot. Ian had stripped off both his shirt and trousers and was clad only in a pair of shorts and thick soled shoes with canvas uppers. His back and arms were bronzed to a smooth, even tan, his muscles firm and strong. Lost in sheer admiration of the man's physique, Vanessa's gaze travelled to his equally brown legs whose calf muscles looked hard as iron. She had never seen such a fine specimen of manhood. She found herself letting out a sigh, and gave herself a mental shake.

Such a smooth even tan with no lines of demarcation at all could have only been acquired by continuous and prolonged sunbathing—possibly on some beach. In all probability he'd been a rich playboy before he bought, or inherited the Lodge, she told herself contemptuously.

But as she worked she could not prevent her gaze from straying in his direction from time to time.

' Cuts quite a fine figure, my brother, doesn't he?' Freda said at once with a mischievous smile.

' He's certainly very tanned,' Vanessa answered as carelessly as she could. ' Where did he get it? The Mediterranean?'

Freda laughed. ' Good heavens, no! Working mostly. Ian always strips off like that when it's warm and he's doing any outdoor work.'

Once again Vanessa was put in the wrong about Ian Hamilton, and she did not like it one bit.

By lunch time quite a large area had been tackled, the unrooted hogweed lying limp and defeated in the sun. Freda had brought enough sandwiches and fruit with her to feed an army, and Nancy laid a table under the shade of the sycamore, adding a great bowl of fresh crisp lettuce and early greenhouse tomatoes, smelling and tasting wonderful. She explained that she had bought them from a neighbour who had his own greenhouse.

'I think I might grow some another year,' Vanessa mused. 'I grew them at home. They're not much trouble when you're around all day to look after them.'

'You mean instead of plants?' queried Ian.

'No, I was thinking of a second greenhouse. And when the tomatoes were finished I could use it for chrysanthemums.'

Freda laughed. 'You talk like a real gardener. I've never known a girl like you.'

But Ian's face was serious. 'Amateur gardening is one thing, building up a paying concern is another—if that's what you want to do.'

'I'm well aware of that,' Vanessa retorted. 'What I want now are some seed boxes and propagating medium and a few packets of seeds. If I can sow them during the next few days, they'll flower in time for Christmas.'

'Such as?' asked Ian in a sceptical tone.

'Such as browalia, exacum, calceolaria and cineraria —though I doubt if *they'll* be ready in time for Christmas, actually,' she added, meaning the two latter flowering plants.

Ian eyed her through lids half closed against the sun as it filtered through the outer leaves of the tree.

'I suppose you know you can buy seedlings at this time of the year? Not as cheaply as packets of seeds, of course, but you'd still make a considerable profit *and* with the right sort of treatment you might well have them coming into flower for Christmas.'

'And what do you call the right sort of treatment?' queried his sister.

His lips curved at the corners. 'Ask Vanessa. She's the expert.'

If he was hoping to catch her out, Vanessa thought, he was much mistaken.

'Well, cinerarias and calceolarias certainly need time to develop a good root system and an adequate period of time outdoors before they're taken into the greenhouse. But if they could be potted singly now in three-inch pots and put outside in a shady place, then about the middle of July potted on in five or six inch pots and into a " cold " greenhouse in the middle of August, they might stand a chance. But it's no good trying to bring cinerarias on by too much heat in the early stages. *Is* there a nursery nearby where I can buy seedling pot plants? I might even get some cyclamen.'

Ian nodded. 'There's a good one just this side of town on the Barnley road. You can get your plants, seeds and everything from them. Why not let Freda run you out there?'

'Would you, Freda?' asked Vanessa.

'Of course,' Freda answered promptly. 'When would you like to go—in the morning?'

'Suits me fine, thanks.'

It was somewhere during the middle of the afternoon that Miles Kendal drove up in his car. Vanessa left her task to go to speak to him.

He surveyed the scene with some surprise. 'What's all this? A village working party?'

Vanessa explained to him and he grimaced. 'Well, I'd wade in and help, myself, but I'm on my way to town and wondered if you wanted to go in for anything.'

Vanessa suddenly thought how she'd love to be able to

prepare some of her seed trays this evening if only she had all the necessary materials.

'There *are* one or two things I need,' she told him. 'Would you be coming straight back? And have you room in the boot of your car for about half a hundred-weight of seed compost?'

He grinned. 'Yes, I think so—and we can come straight back if you must.'

'That's awfully good of you.'

Vanessa went back to Freda and was vaguely aware that Ian had ceased his digging for a moment and was leaning on his spade watching her.

'Freda, do you mind? Miles Kendal is going into town *now* and he's offered to run me to the garden centre. If I go right away I'll be able to do some of my sowing tonight.'

Freda glanced across at Miles, his arms folded, leaning on the bonnet of his car smoking a cigarette.

'No, I don't mind,' she said quietly. 'But if I'd known you were so anxious to get started *I* could have run you there this afternoon.'

'I thought as Miles was going anyway, it would save you the trouble,' Vanessa said uncomfortably.

'It wouldn't have been any trouble. But you go if you want to.'

Vanessa thanked her for all she had done, aware uneasily that neither Freda nor her brother liked Miles. But she reasoned that she couldn't be expected to dislike him simply because they did.

'Nancy will be bringing out some tea before long, I expect,' she added. 'But don't work any more, Freda. I'm sure you've done more than enough. Ian too, but you've both been a great help. It would have taken Joe and me a week to do all that's been done today.'

'Think nothing of it,' answered Freda.

Vanessa hurried indoors to change and to pick up some money. Before she came out again she put a couple of pounds in two envelopes and asked Nancy to give one each to Ian's men. She simply could not have them working for her for nothing. Outside, she braced herself to go and thank Ian, knowing she would meet with his disapproval.

He listened to her thanks and her explanation of why she had dropped everything to go with Miles, his face an expressionless mask, and made no comment whatever. But the coldness of his grey eyes was enough to tell her what his opinion was.

Vanessa walked away from him, her chin lifted defiantly. She had not asked him to come. She had thanked him and she had left money behind for his men. She refused to allow him either to intimidate her or to dictate to her. But she could not put a name to the feeling buried deep within her.

Miles grinned widely as he opened his car door for her. 'Friend Ian didn't look very pleased,' he said.

Vanessa frowned. 'Do you think it was rude of me to have left them? Even Freda didn't seem very pleased —though she said she didn't mind.'

Miles pulled the self-starter before answering. 'Did you ask them to come and give you a hand?'

'No, Ian offered to send a man to put some glass in the greenhouse, but this morning he turned up with *two* men as well as Freda.'

Miles turned the car and set off down the drive. 'I —don't—like—the—sound—of—it,' he said slowly.

She glanced at him swiftly. 'How do you mean?'

'They're trying to get round you, Vanessa, as I said they would. In one way or another they intend to get their hands on your property.'

But Vanessa felt this was too sweeping. 'Oh, I think they're trying genuinely to be helpful, Miles,' she protested. 'In any case I've already told Ian I shall never sell.'

'I don't blame you,' he said, turning the car into the

66

road. 'It's a very desirable piece of land, and it's been a shame to see it going to waste. But purely as a matter of interest, why are you so adamant? The house is much too big for you, isn't it? And why spend all your energies on trying to clear that impossible weed?'

'The weed is not impossible,' she answered, and told him what she had found out about it and her system for getting rid of it.

'That's quite a discovery,' he conceded. 'But it's still a mammoth undertaking unless you want to be dependent on people like Hamilton. Mind you, I'd have been along to give you a hand myself if I'd known you were going to get down to it in earnest.'

She flashed him a smile of amusement. 'But you wouldn't have been "trying to get round me".'

She saw his eyebrows shoot up. 'You know perfectly well that isn't true—at least, not for any ulterior motive. I just happen to like you. What made you say that, anyway?'

'Well, I understand you're a property developer. You'd like to buy my aunt's house and land too, wouldn't you?'

He frowned. 'What do you mean—"you understand"? You knew from the start what my profession was. I gave you my card.'

Vanessa now realized that she had never properly looked at his card. She didn't know what had come over her since she had left home.

'I'm sorry, Miles, I was only joking. But seriously, have you ever made my aunt an offer for Puck's Hill?'

'Of course. Why not? But once she said no, that was that. I didn't try to pressurize her.'

'You haven't tried with *me*.'

He smiled. 'You've already told me you don't intend selling, and that's good enough for me. If you were ever to change your mind, of course, I hope you'd let me know. Which brings me to my other question you haven't answered yet. Why are you adamant about not selling when the place has got so many disadvantages? If you were to sell it, you'd have money to buy *two* houses—or one, and enough money left over to sail half-way round the world.'

She hesitated for a moment, then told him quietly: 'The main reason, I suppose, is because I promised Aunt Maud that I wouldn't.'

'Oh, for crying out loud!' he groaned. 'Death-bed promises! The very worst form of tyranny. You can never be released from them. The trouble is they're usually extracted under abnormal circumstances. Some-times, of course,' he amended swiftly, 'dying people don't really know what they're saying or doing, and I feel sure that was the case with your aunt. That place is going to be a millstone around your neck, but I don't suppose she realized it.'

He had made such an interesting point, and there was so much truth in what he had said that for a moment or two Vanessa sat in thoughtful silence. Miles glanced at her uneasily.

'Don't get me wrong, Vanessa. It's you I'm think-ing of. I've seen this sort of thing happen before. A person makes a last request and the one left behind ruins their entire life trying to keep the promise. And as often as not it's something that isn't remotely worthwhile. Dying people aren't normal, they're not responsible for what they're saying. Your aunt was obviously very fond of you. If she'd been in full possession of her senses when she made you promise never to sell, she would surely have left you some money for the place's upkeep.'

'Oh, but she did. I forgot to tell you.'

'Really?' He sounded more abashed than pleased, but when she went on to tell him the amount, he shook his head. 'But if you don't mind me saying so, that's chicken feed. In fact, it could turn out to be worse than having nothing. It will only encourage you to put a lot of time and effort into keeping your promise and wear yourself out in the process. That's barely enough to live on for more than about three months by the time you've paid your rates, electricity bills and what-have-you.'

She told him her plans for letting the barn and propagating house plants to sell.

'I suppose you'll say all that's chicken feed, too,' she said a little despondently.

He shrugged. 'Well, I don't want to discourage you, but there are no windows in the barn, are there? That means another outlay for you. Only on very hot nights will it be fit to dance with the doors open. Even then you won't find the village people willing to pay more than about ten bob a night for the hire. Maybe in the winter for bingo, yes, but then you'll have to heat the place, won't you? And of course, your pot plants won't be ready for sale for another six months at least.'

Vanessa tried to joke. 'You'll have me in tears any minute!' But she really was beginning to feel like crying.

Miles's hand shot out. 'Pay no attention to me, Vanessa. I didn't mean to put you off. It's just that I'm so concerned about *you*. I could stand in the sidelines and cheer you on. I could give you every encouragement by wading in and helping you as Hamilton and his sister have done, but that wouldn't be doing you any kindness. Quite the reverse. It would be better, in my opinion, if you'd put your aunt's wishes down to the wanderings of a sick woman—and really, Vanessa, she was a little eccentric at best, even you must admit that—and ask yourself seriously whether you really are doing the right thing by hanging on to the place. Sell it to Ian Hamilton, sell it to whoever you like, but don't kill yourself by trying to make it earn money so that you can keep a promise which—who knows—even your aunt might be regretting having asked you to keep—if you believe in life after death.'

Vanessa didn't know what to say to such undeniably common sense. It was true Aunt Maud had been an eccentric. It ran in the family. Was she in danger of following literally in her aunt's footsteps, living in that great house in poverty or at best just earning enough by raising plants to keep the place going and herself in food and bare necessities of clothing? She would probably become just as much a fanatic about her plants as Aunt Maud had been about her birds.

She put the depressing picture behind her as Miles drew up outside the nursery and garden centre.

' I could leave you here to browse and buy what you want, then call back for you in about half an hour, if you like,' he suggested.

' Are you sure I'm not putting you to a lot of inconvenience?' she asked him.

He gave her a smile. ' Quite sure. Half an hour will be ample for what I want to do. But just take your time. I'm in no hurry.'

He drove off and she looked interestedly around. At the entrance attractive flower beds were laid out, and a paved drive led to a large open-plan shop where one could buy absolutely everything one needed for a garden. Vanessa decided she would be a regular visitor here, then realized she had no means of transport without possibly having to take two buses, one into town and another out again, and those only at restricted times. But a car of her own was out of the question.

Knowing how many plants could be had from just one packet of seed, Vanessa did not buy more than two each of the kind she had planned, but as her eyes ran along the packets of seeds in the rack, all kinds of possibilities occurred to her. Her excitement mounting, she reached for one after another of the brightly coloured packets depicting superb, larger-than-life-sized blooms, unblemished either by wind, rain or sun. She must think beyond Christmas to next spring. She would use the barn as a sort of shop where people could come and buy their plants for the garden as well as for the house. There was no end to what she could grow and sell. She would buy a few geraniums and take cuttings, rear some colourful coleus. She simply could not fail.

She bought seed boxes and sowing medium; one pink, one white and one red geranium, then wandered outside to where the boxes of seedlings were hardening off. The man who served her looked at her in surprise mingled with amusement as she bought four dozen cinerarias, calceolarias and cyclamen.

'You starting up a shop?' he asked, nearer the truth than he imagined.

She laughed and said she was buying them for Christmas presents, which was also near the truth. Pot plants as presents were becoming more and more popular.

Miles opened his eyes wide too, when he saw the stack of items she had bought.

'You really mean it, don't you?' he said soberly, shaking his head.

'Well, yes, of course.'

She found his lack of enthusiasm for her scheme rather dampening, though he meant it from the best of motives, she felt sure.

They stacked the things in the car, and Miles drove her home again, but this time in comparative silence. Vanessa sat in silence too—a troubled silence. Would her enterprise be successful? It was all very well being able to rear plants, but supposing not enough people bought them? Had Aunt Maud been right to ask her to promise not to sell Puck's Hill? Miles had made a very good point about 'death-bed promises'. One could never ask to be released from them. Where, she asked herself, did respect for the wishes of a person one has loved end and sheer sentiment take over, and at what

71

point did determination become obstinacy?

Freda and Ian and his men had gone when Vanessa arrived back home. Joe was putting away tools preparatory to going home himself.

'Mr Hamilton said to tell you he'll be along to see you some time tomorrow, miss.'

'Thank you, Joe. Goodnight.'

She asked Miles if he would like some tea. He was eyeing the large area of unrooted weeds and the stacks ready for burning.

'They've done well, haven't they?' she ventured against the speculative expression on his face.

He nodded. 'Hamilton has, at any rate. If he can ever persuade you to sell, having this weed cleared will suit him fine.'

'I suppose so.' She cast him a mischievous smile. 'Tell me, Miles, to what purpose would *you* put the house and land if I sold it to you?'

He looked at her seriously for a moment, then laughed suddenly.

'You've got me there, haven't you? I haven't thought a great deal about it. I can tell you this—I'd put it to a darned sight more practical use than Ian Hamilton would—and to be honest the giant hogweed, or whatever its Latin name is, wouldn't be much use to *me*, either.'

At least he was frank. 'Will you come in and have a cup of tea with me?' she repeated.

'It will be a pleasure.'

She took him into the room which was to become her study/sitting room and left him looking at the book on natural history while she went to make the tea. When she returned he was eyeing some of the other books.

'Dry as dust most of them, aren't they?' he said. 'What on earth are you going to do with them?'

'Sell them. At least most of them. Maybe to private collectors or libraries.'

He smiled. 'So your aunt didn't extract any promise about these—and I take it you've no sentimental attachment to them.'

'Silly, of course not! I shall simply have to use my instinct and my discretion about things.'

He put his hand on her shoulder. 'That's the stuff!'

After tea he suggested they might spend the rest of the evening together.

'A film and supper afterwards—something like that?' he said.

But she shook her head. 'Some other time, Miles, if you don't mind. After leaving Ian and his men doing my work for me, I don't feel justified in going out again now. I must make a start on my propagating.'

He shook his head disapprovingly. 'Doing your work for you, my foot! You're a dear sweet girl and more likely to be put upon than anything else. But what about making a firm date with me? As far as I can see it's the only way I'm going to be able to see you for more than half an hour at a time. If the weather's nice on Sunday we could go out for a picnic lunch.'

'Sorry, Miles, I can't.'

'Why not?'

She sighed, knowing what his reaction would be. 'Freda Hamilton has invited me over there for lunch. I—couldn't very well say no.'

'Couldn't you? There might come a time when you will want to. Are you free on Saturday, then. We could make it a theatre and supper.'

'Yes, all right. Thanks very much.'

She saw him out, then went back indoors to change into her working slacks before tackling the job of filling the seed trays and sowing her seeds, her mind going over some of the things Miles had said, and thinking too about Ian Hamilton. Both men professed to have her welfare at heart, or at any rate, in mind, yet both men wanted Puck's Hill. Which of the two was the more genuine? Miles, who was trying to prevent her from making mistakes and running into failure, or Ian who was encouraging her and helping her?

CHAPTER IV

Vanessa had taken the precaution of picking up some fumigating tablets from the garden centre so that she could sterilize the greenhouse. She wanted to make sure that no disease would attack her plants or seedlings. She sealed up the windows, lit two of the tablets, then closed the door and sealed that from the outside. It was early June, so danger of morning frosts would be over, but as a precaution she erected a trestle table in the large kitchen and put her boxes of seedlings and seed trays there for the night. Tomorrow she would have to transplant some of the seedlings into three-inch pots so that they would better be able to develop strong roots and so make good flowering plants. She must also get Joe to help her to make frames so that they could be stood outside. And she would need peat with which to surround them. This was something she had not thought to bring from the garden centre. If only she had her own transport!

She was digging around beneath some trees the next morning in the hope of finding some natural peat when she saw Ian walking around looking at various things— their work of yesterday, the greenhouse, the frames Joe was constructing and the newly cleaned out barn. Vanessa stood and watched him for a minute or two. *Walking around as if he already owns the place.* The phrase came unbidden into her mind and she felt ashamed. Why did she resent Ian Hamilton so much? True, he was inclined to be high-handed, and he lacked the kind of charm Miles had, but— She broke off her thoughts abruptly. There was something about Ian which both attracted and repelled her.

Then he scanned the garden and saw her, so she dropped the spade and walked towards him.

'I hope you don't mind,' he said, disarming her. 'I hopped over the fence instead of coming round by the road.'

'That's all right.'

His glance went to where she had been digging. 'What are you doing now?' he asked.

She told him. 'It's the one thing I forgot to buy yesterday, and not having my own transport—'

His face became thoughtful. 'You ought to have a car of some sort. It's practically an essential in the country. You can't be depending on the times of buses or—or other people. You should be on the phone, too. Have you thought any more about that?'

She didn't answer for a moment. A certain pride forbade her to keep saying she hadn't the money for these extras. She was about to say that she hadn't really felt a serious or urgent need for either a car or the telephone when he forestalled her.

'If you're going into any sort of business, you simply must be on the phone,' he said. 'And a car needn't cost you the earth. I know where you can get quite a good reliable utility for around a hundred. You could spread the cost over twelve months with very little drain on your capital. As for peat, you never need to buy that. I've got a whole estate full—yours for the taking. In fact I'll send one of the men round with a few sacks full.'

She felt he was thrusting solutions to her problems down her throat. She was not used to other people making her decisions for her.

'Thanks very much,' she said coolly, 'but I have all the peat I want here for the time being. Please don't put your men to any trouble on my account. As to the car and telephone—I'm not in any hurry.'

He drew an exasperated breath and looked as if he might say something explosive, then changed his mind. But his expression was stormy. He pulled two envelopes out of his pockets and handed them to her.

'These are the envelopes you left with money inside for my men yesterday. They don't want payment for what they did.'

'Don't they?' she flashed back. 'Or have they returned it because you told them to?'

His jaw tightened. He drew another deep breath and expelled it forcibly.

'You really are the most difficult person I've ever met in my whole life!'

'And you, Mr Hamilton, are the most—irritating and high-handed that *I* have ever met! Everyone is expected to jump to your commands.'

He stared at her as if she had taken leave of her senses, as if it was incredible that anyone could think such things about him, still less say them.

'I'm sorry,' he jerked out at last, but in a far from apologetic tone, and turned and strode down the drive in long, angry strides.

Vanessa sighed and wished she had better control of her tongue. Ian Hamilton seemed to bring out the worst in her. All the same she smarted for a very long time, his words running round and round in her brain. *You really are the most difficult person I've ever met in my whole life.* How could she possibly go to his house for lunch on Sunday now?

As she half expected, Freda paid her a visit that evening. Vanessa was working late, tackling the weed which flanked the drive. Ian and his men had done quite a considerable amount, but Vanessa felt it was important to get the entrance to the house and barn clear as soon as possible. She was thinking of having some posters printed announcing that the barn at Puck's Hill was available for hire. As well as to earn a little money from the hire, she felt it would get the people of the village accustomed to visiting the place in preparation for the time when her plants were ready.

'Still hard at it?' queried Freda.

Vanessa smiled. She really liked Freda. 'I think I'll call it a day now, at any rate. Come and have a cup of coffee with me.'

She knew what Miles would have said about Freda's visit, and whether it was true or not, she did not care. It was good to have someone her own age to talk to.

'I came to make sure you were still coming to have lunch with us on Sunday,' Freda said when they were drinking their coffee.

'Yes—if you're sure you want me.'

'Of course we do.'

Vanessa smiled ruefully into her cup. 'I'm afraid I was very rude to Ian this morning.'

Freda laughed. 'So was he to you, I gather. You'll have to forgive Ian. He does tend to give the impression of being " in charge ". He doesn't mean to dictate, it's just that he's so accustomed to taking responsibility, and being so fond of your aunt—'

'I'd—rather he didn't feel responsible for me, all the same,' Vanessa murmured.

'He's only trying to help,' Freda pointed out mildly.

'I suppose so, and I appreciate his efforts, really I do, but I didn't want the men to work for me for nothing. Why should they?'

'Well, as to that, Vanessa, they were already being paid by Ian, you see. And the whole idea was to give you a hand and try to *save* you a little money. You'll run out of it all too quickly, you know, if you don't watch out.'

'You make me feel ashamed.'

Freda shook her head. 'No need for that. If you feel so strongly about giving the men something, why not just give them a token payment—about a quarter the amount you did originally, which was almost the equivalent of a day's wages.'

But Vanessa was not quite convinced. 'Are you *sure* the men didn't want the extra money?'

'Quite sure. They brought it to Ian and gave it to him to give back to you.'

'Oh.'

Freda looked at her downcast face. 'Cheer up, we all make mistakes. I should just forget about this morning's little scene, if I were you. Ian won't want to be reminded of it.'

'You're a great peacemaker, aren't you? I'm not usually so pigheaded. I don't know what's the matter with me.'

'It's this house and everything. You've taken on a good deal.'

'Don't make excuses for me,' Vanessa told her. 'I've been as stubborn as can be about the business of getting on the phone. I wasn't *entirely* penniless when I came down here—at least, I had enough money to pay for the installation of a telephone. Of course then, I didn't want to use up my capital on something that didn't seem necessary, but there's been no excuse since finding the money Aunt Maud left me, and I did snap Ian's head off about it. About a car, too.'

'Well, I expect he tried to sell you the idea of having a car before your mind was really ready to accept it,' Freda comforted. 'Anyway, I'll tell Ian to keep on the look-out for one for you. You don't have to have it, if you don't want to. Ian will understand.'

Will he? wondered Vanessa privately. He considered her to be difficult. The most difficult person he had ever met in his whole life. The reminder of it depressed her beyond belief, but she smiled and thanked Freda.

'The telephone is the first step anyway. That will save me having to go to the kiosk and maybe I can get firms to deliver things like sacks of potting soil and pots and so on. Meanwhile, if I want to go into town I can use the public transport.'

Freda pulled a face. 'With two buses a day? And so far apart you have to mill around wasting time instead

79

of being able to come back when you're ready? Look, any time you want to pop into town just let me know. I'll either come in with you or you can borrow my car.'

Vanessa had rarely met such generosity, but she knew the misunderstandings which could arise if one took advantage of such an offer too often or at an inconvenient time. She simply must get a van or small car of some kind before long. She smiled and murmured her thanks, but Freda made a shrewd guess at her thoughts.

'Look, Vanessa. Neither Ian nor I want to force our help on you. We just want you to know you can call on us at any time. We're your neighbours, and we want to be your friends, too. And what are friends for if not to lend a helping hand? So you will let us know, won't you, if there's anything we can do?'

Vanessa had a sudden inspiration. 'You could do one thing for me right away, if you would. Telephone the post office engineer and ask him to come and see me about getting the phone fixed up.'

'I'll do that with pleasure.'

But when Freda had gone Vanessa wondered how far, in actual fact, Freda had been speaking for Ian with regard to their being friends. Freda had done her best to speak peace, but Vanessa couldn't help feeling that Ian was more angry than Freda would have her believe, that he still *was* angry, and had meant every word he had said this morning.

The weather, at any rate, was on Vanessa's side. By Saturday she and Joe had managed to clear of weed several feet on either side of the drive. She wished she dared spend some money on pot grown roses, but she would need so many. She comforted herself with the thought that even bare earth looked better than the rank weed growth. She would have almost forgotten about her date with Miles had not Nancy reminded her when she had been planning at lunch time what to do with the rest of the day. Joe had finished work at twelve as he usually did on Saturdays, and Vanessa thought she would have a change from digging.

'Good heavens, I almost forgot,' she said when Nancy reminded her.

Nancy eyed her shrewdly. 'You can't be very keen if you nearly forgot,' she said.

'Oh, I had been looking forward to going to the theatre,' Vanessa assured her.

'I meant you can't be very keen on Miles Kendal as a person,' pursued Nancy.

'I like him well enough, but that's all. What else?' asked Vanessa.

'What else is there usually, between a man and a woman?' Nancy queried pointedly.

But Vanessa shook her head swiftly. 'I'm not getting any of those kind of notions about Miles Kendal or anyone,' she said firmly. 'And I'm quite sure Miles hasn't any ideas about me beyond ordinary friendship.'

Later on, Vanessa was not quite so sure of that. Not only was he extremely charming and attentive, but over supper he began to talk in wistful terms about a real home of his own.

'I don't mean just a bachelor flat like I have at the moment, but a house and a garden and—well, all that goes with it, like a—wife and children.'

They were sitting side by side at a table and his hand reached out and grasped hers. Just how much significance there was in this, Vanessa dared not think, but she felt the only thing to do was treat him lightly.

She laughed. 'In that order?'

He turned his head and eyed her seriously. 'Let's just say, at the moment, that until—a few weeks ago, I was quite content with my bachelor flat and having a good time.'

Vanessa thought she had better not ask him why a few weeks ago.

'What do you mean by "having a good time"?'
she asked.

His shoulders lifted. 'Well, you know, taking
different girls out, generally living it up. But there
comes a time when a fellow starts thinking about growing roots, if you know what I mean.'

Vanessa tried another tack. 'What about your
parents, Miles? Wouldn't you be happier living with
them rather than on your own?'

He shook his head. 'Heavens, no, not where they
live.'

'Which is?'

'Australia. They emigrated about two years ago, but
I decided to stay here. They sold their house for capital
and wanted me to go with them, naturally, but—well, I
was engaged at the time, and—'

Vanessa knew a swift reawakening of her own only
recently healed wounds.

'Oh, Miles, I'm sorry. What happened?'

'She married someone else, but not to worry. I'm
well over that little episode now. But what about you,
Vanessa? How is it that an absolutely marvellous girl
like you is still free?'

'I suppose because I've still to meet the right person.
Like you I've—had my disappointments.'

'I just can't believe it—a wonderful girl like you.
Attractive, intelligent—'

She laughed. 'Easy on the compliments! You'll
have me getting a swollen head.'

'Not you.'

When he drove her back to Puck's Hill, he seemed in
no hurry to say goodnight. But when she asked him in
for coffee, he declined.

'Let's just sit here and talk for a while. Somehow
that house depresses me.'

Vanessa admitted that it was not very homely. 'But
it will be by the time I've finished with it.'

'I'm sure.' His arm slid across her shoulders and his lips brushed her cheek. 'I'm sure you're a wonderful home-maker, but a house like that was meant for a staff of servants.'

His lips found hers, but Vanessa's mind was too occupied by what he had just said to respond very much. Sometimes she felt Miles was so right, her courage failed her. She pushed against him.

'Please, Miles, if you don't mind, I'd rather go in now.'

Very slowly, he removed his arm. 'I expect you're tired—and no wonder.'

'I am rather—but it's been a lovely evening, Miles. Thank you so much.'

He walked with her to the door of the house and as she was about to say goodnight to him he suddenly put his arms about her and pressed his lips hard on hers. But Vanessa had never been one to indulge in this sort of thing lightly.

'Please, Miles—'

'What's the matter? Don't you like me?'

'Of course I like you, but—'

'But you're tired. I understand.' He put his hands on her shoulders and gave her a long look, a fond smile on his face. 'I can't tell you what this evening has meant to me. When can I see you again? Soon?'

She gave him a faint smile in return and nodded, but felt vaguely uneasy at the change in him. At the present moment, at any rate, she did not want anything deeper than ordinary friendship from any man.

'The G.P.O. are coming to install my telephone on Monday,' she told him evasively. 'I'll give you a ring, then you'll know my number.'

'You—do want to see me again?' he queried, a note of anxiety in his voice.

'Of course. But at the moment, with so much to do, I'd rather not make too many arrangements in advance.

You're always welcome to drop in. But now I really must go in.'

He let her go and she made her way into the house wondering whether Miles always behaved in such a way when he took a girl out for an evening, or whether he was becoming serious about her. She hoped not. She liked him well enough, but that was all.

She slept late the next morning and was awakened by Nancy with a breakfast tray. Vanessa sat up sleepily as the older woman poured out a cup of tea for her.

' This is terrible. It's I who should be doing this for you,' she protested.

' Nonsense. You're working hard. You need someone to " mother " you. In any case, I had my breakfast over an hour ago.'

' Mother me?' Vanessa laughed. ' I never got this kind of spoiling from my own mother.'

' Maybe you didn't work so hard, either.' Nancy looked down at Vanessa, her face serious. ' Are you sure you're doing the right thing by trying to make this place earn money? Don't you think you're taking on too much, doing work which is much too heavy for a woman? You should be thinking of getting married.'

' Married!' For a split second Vanessa experienced small stabs of something like pain. Then she laughed. ' Don't *you* start, Nancy. You sound almost like Miles Kendal.'

Nancy stared at her. ' You don't mean he's asked you to marry him?'

' No, not yet—and I'm not saying he intends to, but he was making some very odd noises last night.'

Nancy shook her head gravely. ' I wouldn't trust that young man any further than I could throw him. No, Ian's the one for you, Vanessa.'

At this everything within Vanessa seemed to freeze. ' Now you're talking nonsense. Ian Hamilton is the very last person I would marry. But there's no need to

84

worry. He is the one person who will never ask me.'

'I'll leave you to eat your breakfast,' Nancy answered, and went out of the room.

Vanessa gave a long sigh as she tackled her toast and honey. Ian Hamilton did not even like her, nor she him.

Dressing to go to the Lodge for lunch Vanessa could not help wishing she had bought more clothes. After changing her mind several times between a dress or summer suit, she chose a dress she had bought last year and which she had scarcely worn, a simple, easy-to-wear dress in white with groups of narrow pleats from neck to hem. She was wondering whether to walk round by the road or pop over the fence dividing the two properties when Freda drove up.

'I thought I'd better collect you,' she said. 'It's a longish walk by road and walking through some parts of the woods can be tricky, especially while there's so much clearance being done.'

Vanessa was consumed with curiosity to see what the Hamiltons' home was like. Freda drove in what amounted to a half circle—left, left through the village, and left again through an open gateway which in the Colonel's time was always closed, along a winding drive flanked with beautiful specimen trees and evergreen shrubs and to the house itself made of red brick and rich cedar which blended together perfectly. Running the entire length of the house was a verandah gay with red geraniums and fuchsia, while the surrounding garden was an absolute picture—smooth green lawns, colourful flower beds, roses and pergolas against a background of trees. Vanessa let out an involuntary exclamation of admiration.

'Oh, Freda, when I think of *my* wilderness!'

'Yours will soon be every bit as nice as this the way you're progressing,' Freda comforted.

'Do you sit out here much?' Vanessa asked as they mounted the wooden steps to the verandah.

'Not really,' Freda told her. 'We prefer the back of the house. Come and see.'

Vanessa had subconsciously geared herself to meet Ian as soon as she arrived, but there was still no sign of him as she followed his sister into a wide, carpeted hall and through a pair of very beautiful glass doors to a large sun-lounge, its sliding doors opening on to a paved patio.

'Oh, how lovely!' cried Vanessa.

A fountain played in a small pool, cascades of colour overflowed from hanging baskets, spilled out of urns and flower troughs, and white-painted garden furniture added a touch of elegance as well as luxury, while inside the sun-lounge were comfortable basket-loungers, palms, ferns and other graceful plants.

'Make yourself at home,' invited Freda. 'I'll just pop into the kitchen and see how lunch is getting along.'

Vanessa sank into one of the lounge chairs, and for a moment or two allowed their comfort to take possession of her, then she rose and went to sit on the edge of the raised pool and watched the goldfish darting like flashes of copper light hither and thither. She trailed her fingers in the clear water, warmed by the sun and became lost in a vague, misty world of dreams, one of happiness and heart's desire, love and peace. Then, without actually seeing him, she became aware of Ian standing a few yards away. She looked up and found him watching her, an odd expression on his face.

'Hello, Vanessa,' he said quietly.

CHAPTER V

Vanessa rose slowly, her gaze riveted to his face. 'Hello, Ian.'

He moved towards her, and the brief moment of something which had been beyond understanding passed.

'You look very charming this morning,' he said in a faintly mocking tone. 'And so relaxed there by the pool.'

Sensing an underlying sarcasm, she chose not to accept the compliment.

'It's so restful and attractive out here, I'm afraid it emphasizes the state of my place.'

'You have the satisfaction of creation still to come,' he answered. 'This place wasn't the way I liked it when—Freda and I first came to live here.'

She noticed the hesitation, as if he had been going to say something and then changed it, and realized how little she knew about Ian Hamilton and his sister.

'Did you buy the place or—inherit it?' she asked.

He stared at her for a moment. 'What made you think we'd inherited it? The previous owner was no relative of ours.'

An unexpected relief washed over her. 'I—don't know why I thought that. This house and the woodlands have always been considered to be a sort of hunting ground and—'

'And you considered me to be a rich playboy,' he finished, as she hesitated, seeking for her next phrase.

'I hadn't really thought much about what you were,' she answered coolly.

'And you're not interested.'

His tone was accusative. 'I didn't say that,' she flashed back at him.

For a moment there was a sharp silence between them,

then as if remembering his duty as host, he relaxed.

'Sit down, won't you, and let me get you a sherry— or is there some other drink you prefer?'

She sat down on the padded seat of the white wrought-iron settee.

'A sherry would be very nice, thank you.'

He went inside, and reappeared almost immediately with a tray on which was a decanter and glasses. He poured out two glasses and handed one to her, then sat in one of the chairs half turned to face her. They sipped in silence for a minute or two, then feeling it was up to her to show some interest in the home of her host and hostess, she asked: 'Was this sun-lounge and patio here when you bought the house or have you had them added?'

'Half and half,' he told her. 'There was a verandah of sorts, but it was rather gloomy and depressing with a tiled roof and a wooden rail around in the real hunting lodge style. The patio was just a neglected yard, the paving cracked and uneven, the various outbuildings bare and ugly. But it had a sunny aspect, and I firmly believe a place in which one can relax is essential. So we had a glass roof and sides put in the verandah, sliding plate glass doors along the entire front, as you can see, and some new floor covering. Then we laid coloured paving slabs out here and covered the outbuildings with either trellis work or decorative bricks. A few plants and climbers did the rest.'

'Not to mention this elegant garden furniture,' Vanessa said wistfully.

'They were Freda's idea. In fact, she bought them. I would most likely have made do with canvas chairs and a home-made table of some kind.'

Vanessa was about to ask him why he and his sister had chosen to live at Barn Hill and why they lived together rather than with their parents, when Freda joined them, and with her a young man with fair hair, wearing slacks and a white open-necked shirt. Freda made the introduction.

'Vanessa, meet a friend of mine, Harry Davidson. Harry, this is our new neighbour, Vanessa Woodrow.'

A very special friend? Vanessa wondered as she shook hands with the young man. At any rate, she felt he would be a welcome addition to the small luncheon party.

The meal was served in the oak-panelled dining room, furnished in the Jacobean period which Vanessa found so mellow and satisfying to look at.

'You like the room?' Ian said, seeing how she glanced around.

She nodded. 'Very much. I like old furniture—or rather, antique furniture.'

'Do I take it you wouldn't settle for the reproduction kind?' he queried.

'I would if it was well made. Why not? It isn't the period in which things are made which counts, but the craftsmanship and design. Did you—buy the furniture in with the house?' she queried, still curious as to why a brother and sister should be living together.

Ian shook his head. 'The Colonel took his furniture with him to the Isle of Wight. All the furniture in the house was chosen at various times by either Freda or myself. Fortunately our tastes don't clash too violently, although Freda prefers the more modern look. If she shows you her own rooms afterwards, you'll see what I mean.'

It was a pleasant and most enjoyable meal. Ian sat at the head of the table looking very much a family man as he carved the Sunday joint, and Vanessa couldn't help wondering why he was still unmarried. Freda, she guessed, would not remain single for much longer, judging from the expressive glances she and Harry exchanged from time to time. But in the event of her marrying, what would happen to Ian? Would he live in this house alone?

Vanessa tried to control her thoughts better. For all she knew Ian might already have someone he was hoping to marry, someone who lived in another part of the country perhaps. But why another part of the country? she asked herself. It could be a girl in the village. She had not known Ian and his sister long enough to know much about them, neither did she know many people in the village. As well as the cottages and terrace houses there were some quite big houses here and there.

'Freda has been telling me what a heroic job you're doing at Puck's Hill.' Harry spoke to Vanessa across the table. She smiled.

'Well, it did seem rather formidable at first, but now I've found a way of tackling that giant hogweed—and thanks to the help I've had from Freda and Ian, it doesn't seem nearly as hopeless. There's still an awful lot of work, though. I've realized that even more after seeing Freda and Ian's lovely house and garden.'

'There's quite a considerable amount of land there, isn't there?' pursued Harry. 'You're not going to try to cultivate it all, are you?'

'I'm aiming to clear the whole area of that hogweed, anyway,' she answered. 'After that, I'm not sure. I might develop my plant growing into a sort of nursery business, or just add more greenhouses and grass the rest.'

'A nursery business? Why not grow trees?' suggested Harry.

An alert glance passed between Ian Hamilton and his sister.

'What sort of trees?' asked Vanessa.

Harry shrugged. 'Oh, any kind. Christmas trees, for instance. Much less trouble than growing roses or whatever it is you have in mind. Ian could—'

The rest of his sentence was cut off short by Freda.

'*Harry*, Vanessa doesn't know you're a forester. He simply can't help trying to sell the idea of trees to everyone,' she explained to Vanessa. 'Unlike Ian, he works for the Forestry Commission, but he's got trees on the brain.'

'Haven't we all,' murmured Ian. 'But Vanessa is more interested in plants and flowers.'

Vanessa wondered what Harry had been about to say when Freda had interrupted him.

'I wasn't thinking of growing roses, actually,' she answered him. 'Just things like perennials—herbaceous border plants and maybe shrubs. But the idea of growing Christmas trees is intriguing. I must think about that.'

After lunch Ian and Harry gallantly said they would do the washing up while Freda showed Vanessa the rest of the house.

'Coffee on the patio in half an hour,' Ian told them. 'So don't get gossiping and forget the time.'

Freda made some tart rejoinder and led the way upstairs. 'I'll show you the kitchen and other downstairs rooms last—when they've done the washing up.'

'Is Ian always so domesticated?' asked Vanessa.

'Oh yes. He calls it a fair division of labour. I do the cooking, he does the washing up—when there's no one else to do it. Our daily help works from nine to four, five days a week. Evenings and week-ends we have to do our own chores.'

It was at this point that Vanessa ventured to ask: 'How does it happen that you and Ian are living together? Are your parents still living?'

'Oh yes,' came the surprising answer. Vanessa had thought perhaps they were both dead. 'They live in Hampshire—the New Forest. Father is a head forester there. It's just that Ian wanted to have his own woodlands and carry on his own forestry business. He bought this place and—I thought I'd like to come too. I wanted a change. In fact I wanted to recover from a disappointing love affair. You know the sort of thing—I was in love, he wasn't, so I thought I'd get away, keep house for Ian and help him with the secretarial work. And I'm glad I did. Because now I've met Harry and he's in love with me and *vice-versa*. A much more satisfactory state of things.'

'Yes, indeed,' Vanessa said fervently. 'And I'm very glad for you. Have you fixed a date for your wedding?'

Freda shook her head. 'Not yet. Ian would hate to hear me say this—but I *would* like to make sure things are going to work out happily for him too. I'd hate to leave him on his own.'

'Is there—anyone?' Vanessa felt encouraged to ask.

Freda gave a little smile, giving a slight shake of her head at the same time.

'I have an idea that there is, but he hasn't said anything, so I just keep on hoping.'

Vanessa wondered who the mysterious woman was and what kind of lover Ian would be, whether he would 'rush a woman off her feet' or gently woo, be jealous and possessive or easy-going. She decided he would be anything but easy-going.

Vanessa loved the house. It had four large bedrooms and two smaller ones, with two bathrooms and a large square landing housing linen cupboards which would be many a housewife's dream.

'Roomy, and at the same time compact,' was her verdict.

'It's a shade on the big side for two, of course,' Freda said, 'unless you do a lot of entertaining—which we don't at present. But it went with the property, and it was a property Ian was looking for primarily. One with woodlands or room to develop. It will be an ideal family house, though,' she added.

Vanessa noticed the way Freda said *will be*, not *would*

be, as if she was a hundred per cent certain of Ian's marriage. As if, indeed, it were a *fait accompli*.

The two guest rooms were simply but extremely tastefully furnished, one in a décor of blue and gold, the other in grey and pink. A guest would sleep peacefully in either room. Ian's room was in muted shades of green with fine Regency furniture, a comfortable armchair, plenty of books—several, Vanessa noticed, on his bedside table, with antique maps and one or two curious wood carvings to add a truly masculine touch. A fascinating room. Vanessa would like to have lingered —to look at some of the book titles, to see the view from the window and to sit for a while in Ian's armchair. Why she didn't know, unless it was the better to know him through his possessions.

Freda's room was completely feminine in pink and white, with light, modern furniture, a white carpet, pink walls and pretty curtains.

' Quite a contrast to Ian's, isn't it?' laughed Freda, then she added: ' I expect Harry's room is essentially masculine. The problem is, whose taste is reflected when one marries? A mixture would probably look awful, neither one thing nor the other.'

Vanessa agreed that this could be the effect. Then she said without thinking how it could be taken:

' For myself, I'd prefer Ian's room.'

It was not until she met Freda's amused glance that she realized what she had said. She felt her cheeks colouring.

' I didn't mean that. What I did mean was, of the two—yours or Ian's, Ian's would be more to my taste. I don't think I'd want a purely feminine room.'

But Freda only laughed. ' It's all right, I know what you meant. But it did sound rather funny. On the whole, I think my home and Harry's will be a mixture. Periods don't really clash if the designs are good.'

They made their way downstairs, and Vanessa thought

the sitting room the most beautiful she had ever seen. The whole tone was so restful. The colour scheme was green and gold with panelled walls and alcoves, and wall lights with twin fittings. At one end there was a grand piano, a sheet of music on the stand as if someone had recently been playing, the easy chairs and settee were commodious and comfortable-looking and there were one or two interesting pieces of fine furniture which could well be Sheraton.

'Who plays the piano?' she asked.

'Ian. He plays quite well. I think he wanted to do it professionally at one time, but for various reasons it didn't work out.'

'Was he terribly disappointed?'

Freda thought for a moment. 'A little frustrated perhaps at the time, but he soon recovered. And now I think he's rather glad. Once an art form becomes a person's job of work, it's no longer a relaxation, is it?'

'I suppose not.'

'At any rate he enjoys playing in what leisure time he can get.'

'Do you think he could be persuaded to play this afternoon? I'd love to hear him.'

'If you're really keen, he might. But he hates playing to an audience who only listens out of politeness.'

The kitchen was used also as a breakfast room and was a joy of varnished timber and copper brightness. A room adjacent which had probably been intended for a breakfast room was set aside for Freda's own use. 'I do my dressmaking and keep all my own bits and pieces in here,' she explained—while Ian had his study. This again reflected Ian's personality, his love of good furniture and a pleasing colour scheme. The house also had a downstairs cloakroom where raincoats and garden coats could be hung and all kinds of articles deposited which would normally make a house look cluttered.

Ian called out that coffee was ready, so they went out

to the patio.

'Well, what did you think of the house?' Ian asked as they settled down to coffee.

'I love it. It's a perfect dream,' she answered. 'If only I could transform Aunt Maud's house to something like it!'

'Oh, you'll get it the way you want it in time,' Freda murmured.

'What sort of place is your aunt's?' queried Harry. 'A rather big rambling house, I suspect.'

'Yes, it is. All sorts of things *could* be done with it, but it will never be the compact, useful size that this house is,' Vanessa said.

'What will you do with it, then? Convert it into flats or something like that?'

Vanessa shook her head. 'I—don't somehow think Aunt Maud would like that.'

Harry gave her a thoughtful look. 'You—er—set a great deal of store by what your aunt would have liked or disliked?'

Vanessa did not quite know how to answer. Neither Freda nor Ian were taking any part in the conversation, but Ian was eyeing her thoughtfully as if waiting to hear what she had to say. But suddenly Vanessa wanted his opinion on the subject on which Miles had been so adamant.

'What do you think, Ian?' she asked him. 'How far should the wishes of the dead influence the lives of the living? How seriously should one take a promise made to the dying?'

His expression became alert, then a slight frown appeared between his brow.

'I very much doubt,' he said thoughtfully, 'whether it's right to make distinctions between the living and the dead. A promise is a promise and should be kept. I don't believe, myself, in making promises unless I intend to keep them.'

'But, Ian,' interposed Freda, 'people often do intend keeping such promises at the time, but—'

'I know. But there *are* people who make them without the slightest intention of keeping them, who make them rashly, or, which is the more usual, make a promise to a dying person in order to placate them in the same way that they tell lies or half truths to children or the sick and the dying. But from whatever motive, a promise should be honoured no matter to whom it was made or under what circumstances.'

Vanessa thought how uncompromising he was. Such strength of purpose was almost frightening.

'On the other hand,' he went on, 'if we're speaking in general terms, I firmly believe that one should never allow tyranny from either side of the grave. If we're speaking specifically of Vanessa and her aunt, I would say that Vanessa should do what her conscience dictates.'

'Oh dear,' Freda said. 'What a heavy burden of responsibility that could turn out to be! Are we to take it, Vanessa, that you—made your aunt certain promises?'

Vanessa nodded. 'I promised her I would never sell Puck's Hill—and I have every intention of keeping my word.'

This brought a swift exchange of glances among the other three. Ian drew a deep breath and knocked out his pipe on the heel of his shoe. There was silence for a moment or two, during which Vanessa experienced a faint feeling of regret that Aunt Maud had not left her house to someone else. She did not wholeheartedly want it.

Harry was the first to speak. 'You know, it's a very debatable point really, whether or not a person should be bound for ever to a promise made to someone who's dying. I don't mean that one should make promises lightly, but they can be made on a wave of emotion such as pity or sorrow, or to give a dying person peace at the last. The dead can impose tremendous burdens on the living—sometimes unwittingly, of course. But is it right for a person to be carrying a burden too great for them? There is a time, surely, when a promise becomes no longer binding?'

'Certainly there is,' agreed Ian. 'And I would suggest that, if the time comes when Vanessa finds that that house *is*, or has become a burden, then she should consider letting it go. Her aunt was far too fond of her to want her to feel that the place is a millstone around her neck.'

He had used the same phrase that Miles had. Was he really hankering after the property for himself?

After they had talked a little more and finished their coffee, Freda suggested that Ian might show Vanessa around the grounds, and sensing that Freda and Harry might like some time alone together, she said she would love it. She did genuinely want to see the place, but somehow did not feel entirely at ease in Ian's company.

He rose and glanced down at her feet. 'Will you be all right in those sandals, or would you like to borrow a pair of Freda's walking shoes?'

But Vanessa assured him that her sandals were not as flimsy as they looked and that she was used to them.

'Mm,' he said disbelievingly. 'Well, we'd better go through the house and out at the front anyway. It's a bit rough round by the sheds.'

He succeeded in making her feel something of a nuisance, and she wanted to retort that she didn't mind whether it was rough or not, but he stood waiting for her to precede him, so she found herself meekly going through the house as he had indicated.

But once outside, her admiration for the beauty of the garden dispelled all raggedness. She gave a huge sigh.

'Oh, Ian, do you think I'll ever have a garden half as lovely as this?'

He didn't answer for a moment, then he said gruffly:

'Of course you will. The main thing is not to try to do too much at once. You need more help, of course.'

But she shook her head. 'I simply can't afford to pay for any more help at present, so I shall just have to be patient. There's a lot I can do towards improving the garden area near the house, anyway.'

'I suppose so,' he answered.

She glanced at his unsmiling face and wondered what was wrong. She so often seemed to displease him. Or was it that he did not really like her very much? She told herself that she didn't much care whether he did or not, that the feeling was mutual. But she knew in her heart that that wasn't true.

Soon they left the garden area and were walking along wide grassy paths beneath mature beeches, oaks and chestnuts. Vanessa's gaze wandered upwards to the leafy canopy.

'I think I'd like to have more trees,' she murmured. 'But of course it takes years and years for them to reach this height.'

'Some trees grow more quickly than others, of course.'

The lines of his face had softened. Evidently it pleased him that she liked trees.

'You—won't have these lovely beeches and chestnuts felled, will you?' she asked.

He smiled faintly. 'Not all of them, naturally. But you mustn't be too sentimental about trees. There's a time to plant and a time to harvest, just as in other growing things. We've done quite a bit of felling already.'

'Yes, I noticed.'

'The main thing is to keep on planting. The area we've felled will be prepared for a nursery bed to receive young plants.'

'Why do you say that? That the main thing is to keep on planting? For commercial reasons?'

'Not entirely, though of course it is my living, and if

one just kept on felling timber and selling it without re-planting, one would soon be out of business. Besides, the country needs timber. But there's something else attached to it. The feeling, or instinct, that for every tree one fells, another should be planted in its place.'

She smiled. 'I like that. It's good. Do you buy plants or sow seeds of trees?'

'Both, at present, but in time I shall grow from seed only. I don't know how much you know about forestry, but not all trees are allowed to reach maturity before being used commercially. Young chestnuts, for instance, are used for fencing, for pit props, and, of course, the thinning of Norway spruce for the inevitable Christmas trees.'

'It all sounds marvellous.'

The arrived, eventually, at the boundary fence of her own land where they stood silent for a moment or two. For some inexplicable reason Vanessa suddenly hated the fence. It was like a barrier, one she did not want. She looked at Ian's grave face and wondered what he was thinking. Then, eyeing the hogweed still to be dealt with, she said:

'I suppose that horrible stuff encroached on your land too?'

He nodded. 'To some extent, but of course we were able to tackle it before it became too rampageous. And in your aunt's time, our men hopped over the fence and cleared a yard or two there to prevent further encroach-ment too soon.'

Viewed from this side of the fence the task of dealing with the monster weed appeared insuperable, and Vanessa felt swamped in her own inadequacy. How long was it going to take her with help from only Joe Simpkins? A long, long time. She was only just beginning fully to realize the enormity of the task she had set herself. Not only that, but the land ought to be productive as soon as possible. Perhaps Ian would like a strip for tree planting. He wanted more land. She could now see it taking her years to cultivate the whole of the estate and develop a full-scale nursery business, employing a lot of labour as she had envisaged, though rather vaguely.

She sighed heavily and voiced some of her thoughts aloud. ' You know, I can't help feeling that this land ought to be put to a better use more quickly than I shall be able to.' Then she had a sudden inspiration. ' Come to think of it, I didn't promise Aunt Maud anything about the *land*—only the house. I suppose I could sell part of the grounds and just keep enough to develop a *small* nursery business.'

His eyes widened swiftly and his glance sharpened. ' That sounds to me awfully like compromise. I'm quite sure that if your aunt wanted you not to sell Puck's Hill, she was referring also to the land. Don't you realize what was behind her request to you not to sell? This land of yours is a very desirable piece of building land. It has road access, it's well drained, it's not too far from a town while at the same time being in pleasant country surroundings, and in addition, building land is at a premium. Before you know where you are somebody like Miles Kendal will slap a block of flats or something here.'

He paused to fill his pipe and Vanessa was so surprised and so staggered by the way he had taken her up that she could not think what to say to him. But before she could say anything he spoke again.

' Oh, I know people need houses and all that, but if some of these property developers have their way " England's green and pleasant land " will soon be anything but green and far from pleasant.'

He struck a match and cupped it in his hands until the flame spread, then lit his pipe, his face granite-like. Vanessa found herself watching him, noticing the strength of his long fingers, his broad forehead, the shape of his nose, his mouth, his jaw.

'Freda tells me you play the piano,' she said suddenly and rather irrelevantly.

He stared at her. 'That's a swift change of subject. Yes, I do, as a matter of fact. Why?'

'I—just thought I'd like to hear you, that's all. I don't know what made me think of it at this moment, but I think it's time we changed the subject, anyway. I shall think about what you've said, of course, and I think maybe you're right about what Aunt Maud had in mind.'

'Well, that's something,' he said. 'Shall we make our way back to the house?'

They walked in silence at first, Vanessa savouring the smell of earth and peat, letting her gaze soar upward into the leafy canopy above, feeling a peace enter her heart once more and a peculiar oneness with the man at her side.

'Do you—play any kind of a musical instrument yourself?' he asked after a little while.

She smiled and shook her head. 'My mother plays the piano. She sings too. Rather well, as a matter of fact, but for some reason or other it was never suggested that I should learn to play—or sing. Perhaps Mother couldn't bear the thought of having to listen to anyone hammering out five-finger exercises. There was always music in the house of some kind, either Mother performing or a record player playing whole operas or symphonies.'

'So you became a listener rather than a performer. And you never at any time wished you could play an instrument?'

She laughed. 'Once when I was still at school I had a go at learning to play the guitar, but I'm afraid I didn't get very far.'

'Why the guitar? Did you want to play pop—just chords—or in the classic style?'

'Oh, not pop. At least, not in particular. The classic style, I suppose, or to accompany folk songs.'

'Why didn't you persevere?' he asked.

She shrugged. 'I don't know. Perhaps it was just a passing phase. The instrument seemed difficult to handle, I couldn't somehow get my hand across the fret or get true notes. It was more difficult to play than I had anticipated. At any rate, I lost interest. I was teaching myself, of course, from a tutor.'

'That's a big mistake. It's always better to have a good teacher.'

When they reached the house she asked him if he would play the piano for her.

'All right,' he said. 'But don't stand over me. Sit in a chair or listen from another room, whichever you like.'

She eyed him mischievously. 'Is it all right if I hum or tap with my feet?'

He smiled then. 'Yes, because then I shall know you're enjoying it and not just listening out of politeness.'

She chose a chair near the window where she could see across the wide sweep of green lawn and the roses now in full bloom. Ian sat down at the piano and improvised at first—some pleasing sounding chords and arpeggios, then he slid into a Chopin waltz followed by a nocturne. His playing was exquisite. Her mother had never played like this. Ian played on and Vanessa felt she could go on listening to him for ever.

'Oh, Ian,' she sighed when he stopped at last. 'Do you think I could ever learn to play like that?'

'You liked it?'

'It was wonderful!'

'It takes practice,' he said. 'But it's worth it. And many of the classics are quite simple to play really. To love music is the main thing.'

'You make me wish I'd learned when I was a child.

Do you think I'm too old now?'

' You're never too old,' he told her, ' but of course the older you get the more difficult it is to learn anything new. Is there a piano in the house?'

' An old upright in the sitting room.'

' Well, why not have it tuned and take some lessons? I can put you on to a good teacher.'

' In town?' He nodded. ' Then I'll have to get myself a car.'

' That would be a good idea,' he said quietly.

There was a silence. Vanessa was remembering that morning when he had put forward the idea of her having a car and being on the telephone and how she had rejected both suggestions. Freda had said he would keep a look-out for one for her, and she was about to mention this to him when Freda came into the room with a tray of tea.

' That was very nice, Ian. I should think you could do with a cup of tea now. You too, Vanessa, after your tramp round the estate.'

' Thanks,' he said absently, and excused himself, saying there was something he wanted from his room.

Freda's gaze followed him for a moment, then she looked at Vanessa with a swift smile.

' You're honoured,' she said. ' Ian doesn't often give a private recital. At least, not until he's known a person for a very long time.'

' He plays beautifully,' answered Vanessa, wondering about his change of mood when she had said she would have to get a car. Was he still holding her rudeness of that morning against her?

Harry came in followed by Ian, and the talk became general. After tea, Vanessa said she must be going. After all, she had only been invited to lunch, not for the rest of the day, she told herself.

' Oh, but you don't have to run away, does she, Ian?' Freda said swiftly.

'Of course not. She can stay for as long as she likes.'

But Vanessa detected a lack of enthusiasm in his voice, and felt sure that Freda and Harry would want some time alone together. This might result in Ian and herself being thrown into each other's company, something from which Vanessa found herself shrinking.

'That's kind of you,' she said. 'But I feel I really must get back. I don't like leaving Nancy alone too much. She's still missing Aunt Maud.'

'Yes, of course,' murmured Freda.

Vanessa insisted that she could walk back to Puck's Hill by way of the woods and the boundary fence and was glad that Freda and Harry walked part of the way with her instead of Ian. In spite of the odd moments when they seemed to find a common bond, she felt more sure than ever that he disliked her.

But when she arrived home, she sat down at Aunt Maud's old piano, Ian's playing still touching her heart, his strong fingers sometimes caressing the keys, at others commanding them.

The following day her telephone was duly installed, and she rang Freda to tell her what the number was. But it was answered by a voice which Vanessa knew at once was not Freda's. It was that of a young woman with a refined accent which had a strong hint of haughtiness.

'Freda is not here at the moment,' came the voice, in answer to her query.

'Mr Hamilton? Er—Ian?'

'Mr Hamilton is busy. Can I take a message?'

Feeling curiously shut out, Vanessa gave her telephone number and rang off. She wondered who the girl could be, whether a friend of Freda or of Ian, and the speculation occupied her mind so much on and off that she completely forgot to ring Miles to tell him what her number was. He called to see her about mid-week, however.

'Didn't the G.P.O. come?' he asked.

Her hand flew to her mouth. 'Oh, Miles, I'm terribly sorry. Yes, it's all fixed up. I was going to ring you the same evening, but something put me off and then I forgot.'

He waved an admonishing finger at her, then kissed her swiftly.

'I'll forgive you this time. I know you have a lot of things on your mind. I came to ask you if you'd like to go to a dinner and dance. I've got two tickets.'

'Oh, yes. Lovely. Thanks very much. What's the occasion?'

'It's the annual "do" of the Foresters' Club.'

Suddenly she felt deflated. Neither Freda nor Ian had rung her to tell her about this.

'Do you belong?' she asked.

'No, but I have a pal who does. He usually wangles invitations for me if I want them. I expect the Hamiltons will be there, but I don't suppose you mind that.' He eyed her keenly. 'I've never actually asked you. How do you like those two? You had lunch with them on Sunday, didn't you?'

Vanessa led the way into the sitting room before answering. 'I like them both quite a bit. Why shouldn't I?'

He shrugged. 'As I've told you before, I can't stand Ian at any price. You're not seriously telling me that he's made any kind of hit with you?'

She shook her head swiftly. 'I didn't say that. He's not as easy to get along with as Freda is, but I think he's a—man of good character and all that. One you could trust.'

Miles gave a grunt of derision. 'I wouldn't be too sure about that if I were you.'

And afterwards, Vanessa did not feel quite so sure. Neither Ian nor Freda had told her about the Forestry Club dance. Why? They had not rung her either, she thought rather miserably. She hardly expected Ian to do so really, although he had been keen enough for her to get on the telephone.

The day after Miles's visit, Freda called. As the weather was still holding good, Vanessa was working outside, digging up more of the hogweed, wondering whether there would ever be an end to it, feeling, on the whole, a little discouraged.

'Poor you,' sympathized Freda. 'You've set yourself an enormous task.'

Vanessa sighed. 'I doubt whether I'm going to stay the course.'

'You will,' encouraged Freda. 'But you mustn't try to do too much of it at once.' She paused and looked troubled for a moment or two, then she added swiftly: 'But I came to find out if you're on the phone yet. Did the G.P.O. men come on Monday?'

Vanessa frowned. 'But I rang you. I don't know who it was who answered the phone, but you weren't in, and Ian was busy. I did leave a message.'

'Really? Our daily didn't say anything, and I haven't seen any message on the pad. Anyway, I came to ask you if you'd like to come to a dinner and dance.'

Somehow, Vanessa did not think it had been the daily help who had answered the telephone, but she decided not to pursue the matter.

'Is it the Foresters' dinner-dance?' she asked.

'Why, yes. Didn't I tell you about it?'

Vanessa shook her head. 'Miles came yesterday and invited me. He has two tickets.'

'But they weren't available until last night at the meeting, and he wasn't even there. He isn't a member.'

'He has friends.'

'Obviously. And did you accept his invitation?'

Vanessa nodded. 'I hope you don't mind.'

'We—ll, it would have been nice to have you in our party, but never mind. We'll see you there. By the way, we proposed you as a member last night. Meetings are held once a month over the Stag—a lovely old pub just the other side of town. Most times we just talk and have drinks, sometimes we dance, and occasionally we have a speaker. They're good fun, the meetings, I mean, and you meet some interesting people.'

'I'm sure. Thank you very much.'

Freda eyed her quizzically. 'You *are* pleased? I mean—you *did* want to join, didn't you? We don't want to force you into anything.'

'Of course I'm pleased. It's very kind of you and I shall look forward to getting to know a few people.'

It was difficult to explain, even to herself, this leaden feeling inside her. It was somehow tied up with Ian. It was Freda who was setting the pace, offering friendship, taking the initiative. Without prompting from Freda, he would undoubtedly want very little to do with her. Why the thought should depress her, she didn't know. She told herself how ridiculous and how futile such thoughts were, but she still continued to think about Ian and to be depressed every time she did so.

On the night of the dinner and dance Vanessa wore a new dress she had bought recently. She and Freda had driven into town together for a day's shopping and Vanessa had bought a sleeveless dress in silvery blue with a matching jacket. But she dressed without enthusiasm and with an odd feeling in the pit of her stomach. Miles called for her and his admiration of her appearance was unmistakable.

'You look terrific,' he said spontaneously. 'I'll have to keep a tight hold on you, I can see.'

She laughed. It was nice to be flattered. She felt she needed it.

The members of the Foresters' Club and their guests were seated at tables for four, six or eight. Doubtless by prearrangement Vanessa was at a table for six with Miles and two other couples whose surnames were misheard or quickly forgotten in the use of first names. Vanessa did not much care for them. They made a great deal of noise and drank too much, and the girls were dressed in what Vanessa considered to be in shocking taste. She sought the tables until she saw where Freda and Ian were sitting. They were at a table for four, with Harry, naturally, and a girl Vanessa had never seen before. In contrast to the two girls at Vanessa's table this girl was dressed with impeccable taste in white. She was also very beautiful.

Between courses there was dancing. Vanessa danced with each of the other two men in turn and hated it. Both held her too closely. Miles and she were sitting at the table alone when Vanessa's attention became riveted on Ian dancing with the beautiful dark girl in white. Suddenly she found herself in the grip of the fiercest jealousy.

CHAPTER VI

Miles looked at her face. 'What's the matter?'

She started and shifted her gaze back to him. 'Nothing.'

He gave an amused smile and glanced in the direction of Ian and his party.

'If looks could have killed, Cecile would have been stretched out on the ground.'

'Don't be silly. How do you know I wasn't casting venom at Ian? I've never even met—Cecile, did you say her name was? Who is she, anyway?'

Miles gazed across the room through narrowed lids, still wearing the same smile of amusement.

'She is Cecile Harland, daughter of Sir Walter and Lady Harland who live at Kelsley Hall.'

Vanessa frowned, trying to think, trying to shake off the effect of that awful feeling of pure jealousy which had held her momentarily in its grip.

'I—thought Lord Kelsley lived there.'

He shook his head. 'Not now. You're out of date, my love. As a matter of fact she and her parents moved into the area about a month before Hamilton and his sister. They say he followed her here.'

'You mean—'

Miles laughed shortly. 'Because he wanted to marry her, I suppose. I don't think he's had a lot of luck—so far. But he's nothing if not a trier.'

Vanessa supposed vaguely that she ought to hate Miles, but his sneers somehow went over her head. She was looking at the two again, Ian and the beautiful girl, their steps matching perfectly, the rapt expression on Ian's face, the cool detached demeanour of Cecile.

Miles's hand touched Vanessa's. 'Come on, let's dance. Sitting looking at those two is giving me the willies.'

Vanessa rose, feeling something of the 'willies' herself, though she would not have expressed it in quite those terms. She felt like an actress who, for the time being, must keep her own affairs somewhere deep inside in a dark secret place. But what she had felt at the sight of that girl in Ian Hamilton's arms was like a monster which was trying to rear up. *Why did I feel like that? Why? Why?* went round in her brain as Miles swung her round on the dance floor. Ian was nothing to her. Nothing.

When the dance was over, Miles led her back to their table, his hand still clasping hers, and she made no effort to break free. The other two couples, laughing loudly, also came back to the table and Vanessa forced herself to join in their laughter.

Glancing to where Ian and his party were sitting Vanessa noticed Freda and Ian talking animatedly. They looked as though they were having an argument. Ian shook his head, Freda put her hand on his arm, but Ian shook his head even more vigorously. Then suddenly Freda pushed back her chair.

Vanessa turned to answer something Miles was saying to her, but the next moment Freda was standing beside their table. She spoke briefly to the others, then looked at Vanessa.

'We'd all like you to come and have a drink with us, if you will—and if Miles doesn't mind.'

The meal was now finished, and here and there people were moving from one table to another to greet other friends and mix more generally.

Miles's shoulders lifted. 'It's up to Vanessa, of course.'

Vanessa glanced across at Ian. Why had he been shaking his head so vigorously? Had she been the cause of their argument?

'I—don't really think I'll come, Freda, thanks,' she

said.

Freda looked upset. 'But, Vanessa, why? Oh, please—'

At this Vanessa wavered. She liked Freda. The last thing she wanted was to be rude or give offence. She stood up.

'I don't really think *Ian* wants me to.'

'Nonsense, of course he does. He'd have come to fetch you himself except that he can't stand Miles,' Freda said in a low voice. 'And but for a mistake you'd probably have been with our party, wouldn't you? In any case, once the dinner is finished everyone moves around and mixes a bit.'

It seemed churlish and unfriendly to hold out any longer. Vanessa made her excuses to Miles and the others and went with Freda.

Ian and Harry rose politely. It was Freda who introduced the other girl.

'Vanessa, this is an old friend of ours,' she said, confirming something of what Miles had told her. 'Cecile Harland. Cecile, Vanessa is a new friend—and our neighbour.'

'How do you do,' Cecile said in a cool voice.

Vanessa responded in similar fashion, and Ian brought up a chair for her. He ordered drinks and there was a little general conversation in which Cecile took no part, smoking a cigarette in a long holder and looking a trifle bored. Freda and Harry did most of the talking. Ian listened and answered when referred to. Vanessa noticed he had replaced his more usual pipe for a cheroot.

After a while Harry asked Cecile if she would care to dance. As they left the table, Ian half rose in politeness and subsided again. There was a moment or two of silence which Vanessa found uncomfortable, then Ian stubbed out the remains of his cheroot and turned to Vanessa.

'Will you dance?'

She had no option, socially, but to accept, though she felt sure he had only asked her out of courtesy. For a minute they danced in a silence which Vanessa sensed was as strained for him as it was for her, then he said, surprisingly:

'You're looking very charming. Are you enjoying yourself?'

Was he being polite again? Well, she could be too. 'Thank you. Yes, I'm enjoying myself enormously. I'm with a very lively crowd.'

'Yes,' he said briefly.

She looked at his face and saw the granite-like expression.

'You don't like Miles very much, do you?'

'Do you?' he threw back.

She shrugged and lifted her chin defiantly. 'Yes, I do. Why not?'

'No reason at all as long as you don't let your heart rule your head,' he answered.

'And what do you mean by that?'

'I mean that if you have any business dealings with him, be sure not to take his word for anything, but to have it all in writing.'

An unreasonable anger took possession of her. 'You're the most disagreeable man I've ever met in my entire life! I'm not likely to have any " business dealings " with Miles. We're friends because we like each other. I find him courteous, considerate, amiable and —all the things that you are not.'

'Thank you,' he said icily. 'Then I suggest you go back to him.'

'With pleasure.'

She tried to break free, but grim-faced he held on to her until the music stopped.

'Don't make a fool of yourself into the bargain,' he said cuttingly.

Vanessa made her escape to the powder room without answering him. He was hateful, hateful! She just didn't want any more to do with him. But it was a struggle to keep the tears away. She had been hateful too. She knew it. She wasn't enjoying the company of Miles's rowdy friends one bit. She would much rather have been with Freda and Ian.

She forced herself to put a stop to her thoughts, to calm herself and return to her party and Miles. He was alone at the table, waiting for her, and she blessed him.

'What's up?' he asked. 'I saw you dash away looking as though you were seeing red. Friend Ian been his usual pleasant self?'

'You could say that, I suppose. Let's dance, shall we, Miles?'

'Sure.'

He rose eagerly and Vanessa could not help but feel warmed towards him. Later in the evening when it happened that Ian was dancing with Cecile, Freda beckoned Vanessa over.

'What made you leave us so soon?' she asked.

'Don't ask me, Freda. I told you Ian didn't want my company. We—we just don't get along together, that's all.'

Freda shook her head in bewilderment. 'I simply can't believe it.'

'It's true,' Vanessa told her. 'Just because I said I liked Miles and was enjoying myself, he suggested I should go back to him.'

'Is that all? I mean—is that all that happened?'

Vanessa realized she was not being quite fair to Ian. 'Well, I did rather lose my temper.'

Freda smiled. 'You *are* a pair of idiots! I knew something was wrong. Ian's been like a bear with a sore head.'

Vanessa rose swiftly as the music stopped.

'No, don't go—' Freda said quickly.

'I'm sorry, Freda, I must. Give me a ring, or drop in to see me some time.'

Vanessa was thankful when, at last, the evening was at an end. Miles drove her home, and was all she had told Ian that he was—and more. He was not only charming, he was kind and understanding. When Vanessa thanked him and said she had enjoyed the evening, he put his arm around her shoulder and fondled her ear.

'You've only enjoyed it in patches, though, haven't you, Vanessa? What with Ian Hamilton upsetting you and the rowdies we were with.'

'But they didn't "upset me"', she protested, beginning to feel like a person who was hard to please.

'I didn't mean they upset you, altogether, but they weren't quite your type and I must admit they got on my wick at times. We'll have to go there again some time—on our own.' He leaned over and kissed her cheek. 'I must say you looked absolutely great. Not only that, you danced like an angel.'

She blinked, feeling a ridiculous desire to weep. But she said lightly: 'Or do you mean like a fairy?'

'I mean I think you're wonderful. But I mustn't keep you from your beauty sleep—unless of course you had ideas of inviting me in?'

'Not tonight, Miles, if you don't mind. It's very late.'

'Of course I don't mind,' he said gallantly. 'I only mentioned it because I didn't want to pass up a chance of prolonging the evening, if there was any such possibility. Give me your key and I'll unlock the door for you.'

She handed it to him and he helped her out of the car, unlocked the door of the house for her, kissed her lightly and said good-night.

'Good-night, Miles. Come and see me soon.'

'You bet!'

When he had gone she put out the lights and went straight upstairs to her room, thinking how sweet he was. How could Ian be so nasty about him?

At the very thought of Ian tears filled her eyes, and suddenly she felt heartbroken. She stood for a moment, her hand over her mouth as if to stem the tide of emotion which threatened to erupt from deep inside her. She took a few deep breaths. This was ridiculous. She was over-tired, that's what it was. She didn't care two hoots about Ian Hamilton. She wasn't really concerned what he thought of herself or anyone else. She thoroughly disliked him. He managed to spoil every occasion at which he was present, so far as she was concerned. She was determined not to allow him to upset her.

Unconsciously she lifted her chin and resolutely began preparing for bed. She would not think another word about him. She did not run a bath for fear of waking Nancy, but she washed and splashed tepid water liberally on her face. That was better. A hot drink and a book and she would be asleep in no time.

But putting him out of her mind did not prove so easy. It was not that she thought about him consciously but his name seemed to be written indelibly across her brain. He was something which had happened to her. He was a part of her. Yet she did not try to analyse any of this. She only knew that, even when she almost dropped off to sleep with her light still on, he was still in her mind.

Following the events of that evening she plunged herself even more energetically into the work of clearing the grounds of weed and of planning a future business. She talked things over with Nancy.

' You know, I think I'm being too timid for a prospective business woman. I need to be more bold. After all, you have to spend money to make money.'

' What had you in mind?' asked Nancy.

' Windows in the barn, for one thing. And electricity

for future lighting and heating.'

'For the purpose of letting?'

Vanessa shook her head. 'I've been thinking. I won't let the barn after all. I shall want it for plants, and if I try to use it for two purposes I shall run myself into difficulties having continually to move things. Besides, once I start letting it it wouldn't be fair to discontinue. No, I'm going to buy more plants and garden supplies and go into business as soon as possible. Puck's Hill Garden Centre. How about that, Nancy? I can have some posters printed and ask the local shops to display them. In return I could give them a flowering pot plant or fern or something to decorate their shop or house.'

Nancy thought the whole idea was wonderful. 'And why not let's serve teas in the garden when it's nice? In fact there'll be room in the barn for a few tables in wet weather, as well as the plants. I'm not much of a hand with plants, but I could serve tea and cakes. I think it would make a pleasant afternoon or evening for people—especially at the week-ends. They could stroll round the garden, have tea and then buy a plant or so. We hope,' she added.

'Nancy, that's it!' Vanessa cried excitedly. 'That's exactly what we'll do. You're sure it won't be too much for you? I'm afraid you're doing most of the housework too.'

'Of course it won't be too much. It will only be for about a couple of hours in the afternoon. But if anybody comes in the mornings and asks for a coffee—or in the evenings even, well, they can have one. Once we've got it all organized, it won't be any trouble at all. As for tables and chairs, I'm sure we'll find plenty of both in the attic and various rooms.'

'You're a tonic, Nancy. I'll get on to the nearest builder about windows right away. Then the next step will be garden supplies—plant pots, lawn seed—all kinds of things. And some plants already in flower like dwarf chrysanthemums, geraniums and pelargoniums. Foliage plants too. If only I had a car!'

'I thought Ian Hamilton was going to put you on to one?' queried Nancy.

'He did say so, but—' Vanessa shrugged. 'I expect he's waiting for me to *ask* him.'

'Well, why don't you?'

Vanessa's lips tightened and she shook her head. 'I'm not asking *any* favours of Ian Hamilton. He doesn't like me and I don't like him.'

Nancy looked at her in astonishment. 'But what has happened? I was wondering why he hadn't dropped in lately.'

'Nothing's happened,' Vanessa told her. 'We just rub each other up the wrong way, that's all.'

'And what about Freda?' asked Nancy quietly.

'Oh, Freda's all right.'

That same afternoon Nancy came back from a visit to the shops to say she had seen Freda in the chemist's.

'She told me to tell you that she's going into town in the morning, if there's any shopping you'd like to do.'

'That's an odd coincidence,' mused Vanessa. 'I want to go to the garden place. You didn't tell her I wanted to go, did you—I mean before she asked you to give me the message?'

Nancy shook her head vigorously. 'Of course not. She also said she'd been extra busy, that's why she hasn't been round to see you.'

It was nearly a week since the Forestry Club dinner and dance. Miles had dropped in once, but she had neither seen nor heard from Freda or Ian. But Nancy supplied an answer to that, so far as Freda was concerned.

'She says she's rung a couple of times but could get no reply. I told her I was probably shopping and you'd be busy in the garden.'

'You seem to have had quite a chat.'

'I wouldn't say that. I saw Miles Kendal too, but he didn't deign to speak to me.'

'Perhaps he didn't see you,' suggested Vanessa.

'Of course he did.'

Vanessa said no more. Nancy did not like Miles, but she was as prejudiced in Ian Hamilton's favour as Aunt Maud used to be.

Miles called to see her that evening and over a cup of coffee, Vanessa told him about her new plans.

'I rang a local builder, and he can send a man to start on the windows for the barn tomorrow.'

He gave her a wry smile. 'Determined to make a go of it, aren't you?'

'If I can, yes. I must admit I wavered once or twice, but this new plan is the right one, I'm sure.'

'And what are you going to do with all the rest of the ground—if you ever get it cleared?' asked Miles.

'What I don't need for growing on perennials and other plants I shall just grass over. I did have the idea of selling part of the grounds, but—'

'You what?' asked Miles in a startled voice.

Vanessa laughed. 'Calm down! I decided against it.'

'Why? It sounds like a marvellous idea to me, as you're so determined never to sell the house. It would be a jolly good way around the problem.'

But Vanessa shook her head firmly. 'It was pointed out to me that I'd be compromising on my promise to Aunt Maud, and I saw the truth of it.'

Miles frowned. 'Who pointed that out, for heaven's sake? Ian Hamilton?'

'As a matter of fact, yes.'

'He would. Maybe he thinks you should give it away.'

'Hardly. You have given me an idea, though, Miles,' she said, her voice quickening. 'I could lease a piece of it.'

But this idea did not please Miles at all. 'Lease it! You mustn't do that,' he said agitatedly.

'Why not, for heaven's sake?'

'But why do you want to?' he countered. 'You're getting rid of the weed all right now that you've found out what it is, and you've got quite a nice area cleared already.'

'I know. But it's so slow and such hard work. It's not that I mind the work, but while I'm spending day after day on that I'm not able to do anything else. The idea with our Garden Centre is that people can spend a pleasant half hour or so walking around the grounds if they want to. At the moment it's a case of " tiptoe through the hogweed ".'

Miles frowned thoughtfully. 'I admit it's slow going for you. If I'd known you wanted it doing in such a hurry I'd have waded in and helped you.'

'I wasn't in any particular hurry for clearing it down at the farthest end, but now I want to speed things up a bit, and I thought if I could let some out to—'

She broke off. The mention of Ian's name to Miles would be as a red rag to a bull and one on which she did not want to dwell herself. Before the evening of the Foresters' Club affair she would have been quite happy for Ian to use part of her land for the planting of seedling trees, in which case he would have been willing to clear the ground himself. But now she was not sure she wanted any more contact with him than she could help.

'Look,' Miles said earnestly, 'I think your scheme is great, and if I were you I'd hang on to every last little bit of your land for your own purpose. Now I know you want it cleared quickly, I can get hold of some men for you. They'll dig more of this hogweed out in a day than you and Joe can in a week. In fact, for a little bit extra, as you're prepared to spend a pound or two, they'd come Saturday and Sunday and have the lot cleared.'

'In one week-end?' queried Vanessa doubtfully.

'Yes, in one week-end. You'll see. And I'd throw my little bit of an effort in for good measure. But these fellows I know are used to digging. Then when that little lot is cleared, you could get a local contractor in to level the site, have turf laid—and Bob's your uncle, it's all finished.'

Vanessa laughed, feeling suddenly as though a heavy load had been taken off her back.

'Oh, Miles, that would be wonderful. You make it all sound so easy. Can you get your men for this coming week-end, if it's fine?'

'Nothing easier,' he assured her. 'They'll be only too glad to earn a few extra pounds, and I'm sure the week-end will suit them all right so long as they can toddle off to the local in the evening. In fact, if you can lay on beer and sandwiches for lunch they'll work even better.'

Vanessa gave a sigh of relief. 'Miles, how can I ever thank you?'

Miles kissed her cheek. 'Don't thank me, darling girl. I—would do anything for you, you know that.'

At the warmth of her smile he took her in his arms and kissed her. Something stirred within her and she wondered if she was falling in love with him. Why couldn't Ian be more like this—gentle, loving? she found herself thinking.

Whatever feelings had been stirring up for Miles now began to fade, and she stirred in his arms.

'What's the matter?' he murmured.

'I don't know. Too many things still on my mind to be able to relax properly, I suppose.'

He put his hand under her chin. 'Can't you "cast care aside " for a little while? I thought you were just beginning to like me a little.'

'I do like you—'

'Well then—'

Again Miles covered her mouth with his, but still the thought of Ian intruded.

'Miles, don't!' she said sharply.

He let her go with a sigh. 'Not angry, are you?'

She shook her head. 'No. At least, not with you.' Even when he was far away Ian Hamilton could cast a blight.

'Who, then?' queried Miles. 'Someone bugged you and you can't get it out of your mind?'

She nodded. 'But I want to. Let's go out somewhere, Miles, if it's only for half an hour.'

He agreed readily. 'Tell you what. We'll drop in at the Gainsborough House Country Club. It's a nice drive out and a very pleasant place.'

'Are you a member?'

'Well, yes. These places are springing up all over the place, you know. One-time large houses, rather like yours, converted. Belong to one and the membership card admits you to any of them. You don't necessarily have to dine.'

It was a pleasant evening. The trees were all in full leaf and still a fresh, unsullied green. Wheat and barley in the fields grew strongly, giving hope of a good harvest, and roses in the gardens of the villages through which they drove were at the height of their beauty. All the peace-giving, satisfying sights of the countryside, and yet there was a small core within Vanessa which remained unsatisfied, restless.

Miles turned to smile at her. 'Feeling more relaxed now? It's a wonderful evening.'

'Yes, lovely,' she agreed automatically.

Gainsborough House was of the Georgian period, standing white, square and solid in neat, landscaped grounds. A good many smart cars stood in the gravelled driveway, and Vanessa simply could not see Puck's Hill in the same role, no matter how she stretched her imagination.

Inside, the place was as well carpeted and polished as one would expect. Miles led her into a pleasant room from which, through a wide archway, could be seen part of the restaurant. A concealed loudspeaker played light music just loud enough to be heard without intruding on conversation, and the room contained chintz-covered two-seater settees and armchairs. At one end there was even a grand piano.

'Like it?' asked Miles as they chose one of the settees.

'Very much. It's more like a drawing room.'

'That's the idea. Home from home, as it were. You could have done the same with your place if you'd had the money. The archway leading into the restaurant is repeated in there—obviously where several rooms have been knocked into one.'

'Interesting. Does—anyone ever play the piano?' she asked, quite unable to prevent herself thinking of Ian Hamilton.

'Sometimes. Mind you, although you can relax here, it isn't to everybody's liking. It's too quiet.'

She smiled. 'Too quiet for you, Miles?'

A waiter brought them their drinks and Vanessa sat back, thinking that the quiet dignity of this room, at any rate, was very much to her taste.

'No—o. Of course, it depends on the mood I'm in or who's with me. There *are* times when I feel like being lively, but—' he covered her hand with his and turned his head, smiling into her eyes, 'when I'm with someone like you, soft lights and sweet music are ideal. The only trouble is, there are too many people in sight. I want to take you in my arms and kiss you.'

His face was very close to hers as they leaned their heads back on the settee. Vanessa was about to make some light, jesting remark, but the words died in her throat as through the archway came Ian Hamilton with Cecile Harland. Vanessa's smile faded, then she forced it back again and turned to Miles.

122

'Do you see who I see—just coming from the restaurant?'

Miles glanced swiftly across the room, then laughed briefly. 'Well, well! It's beginning to look as though he's got her hooked again.'

Vanessa winced. 'I hope they're not going to stay long.'

'Darling, we'll go if they bother you. I can't stand the sight of him myself.'

Vanessa would not put her own feelings as strongly as that. All the same— Looking round the room for a suitable place to sit, Ian caught sight of Vanessa and Miles. He stared for a moment, his eyes flitting from one to the other, then he nodded coolly and led his companion to a corner seat out of line of Vanessa's direct vision.

'There seems no getting away from the man,' Miles said, almost echoing her own thoughts. 'But let's not bother about him. I want to whisper sweet nothings in your ear. You're very beautiful, do you know that?'

Vanessa laughed briefly. ' " Beauty is in the eye of the beholder ",' she quoted.

'That's only partly true,' he murmured. 'You *are* beautiful—in every way. But you're especially lovely to me.'

She tried not to take him too seriously, not being certain how much in earnest he was, but there was a part of her which wanted very much to feel a man's arms about her. She shook off the feeling by leaning forward and picking up her glass from the table.

'I think you're very nice, too,' she told him lightly.

He reached for his own drink. 'Well, that's a start. Here's to future progress.'

She deliberately avoided looking in the direction of Ian and Cecile Harland, but when Miles suggested another drink, she said she would rather go home, and it was when they were leaving that she discovered the other couple had left without her noticing. At least, they were no longer in the corner.

'They didn't stay very long, did they?' commented Miles. Then he added: 'I should think those two just about deserve each other. She's an out-and-out snob and he'd like to be a gentleman, but isn't. His sister treats him like a tin god because that's what he thinks he is.'

Vanessa did not argue with Miles. He was so very nearly right.

Freda drove up to Puck's Hill in her shooting-brake about half past nine the following morning.

'I thought we might have lunch in town,' she said. 'What about it?'

Vanessa hesitated, feeling she really ought not to spare the time, but as Freda was being kind enough to run her to the garden centre—

'Thanks, that would be nice. I'll just go along to the kitchen to tell Nancy.'

As they were driving along, Vanessa thought what a very useful type of vehicle this was.

'I really must look out for a car like this,' she said. 'That space at the back is ideal for what I want, especially with the back seat hinged back.'

'Er—how would you like to have this?' asked Freda. 'I am thinking of selling it, as a matter of fact. I want a smaller one—a car, not a shooting-brake.'

'Are you sure?' Vanessa asked. It sounded too good a coincidence to be true.

'Yes, quite sure,' Freda assured her. 'We did have a use for it at one time, but not now. I was going to mention it to you, but as it happens, you forestalled me. As far as I'm concerned that space at the back is wasted.'

Vanessa asked what kind of price it would be, and Freda mentioned what sounded a ridiculously low sum.

'I simply must pay you a fair price for it,' she protested.

'And what would you call a fair price?'

'I'm not sure, but—'

'Look, Vanessa, if I let it go in part exchange for another, I shall get very little indeed for it. Much, much less than I'm asking you. I doubt if I'd get a great deal more if I sold it to a local dealer or advertised it. So won't you take it off my hands and stop worrying? If you don't want it, of course, that's a different matter.'

Vanessa did want it. 'I was just making sure you weren't losing money on it on my account. I'll be glad to have it. As soon as you get your new car let me know and I'll make you out a cheque.'

At the garden centre Freda was staggered at the amount Vanessa bought. Vanessa had a word with the proprietor and he had agreed to let her have all she wanted at special prices. He said her place was far enough away from his not to affect his trade. Later, if her own garden centre became successful, she could begin to buy things like tools and other supplies direct from the manufacturers.

'What on earth are you going to do with all this stuff? I though you were only going to sell plants?' Freda asked in a surprised voice.

'I've had a change of plan,' Vanessa told her, and enlarged on her idea.

'But isn't it going to eat into your bit of capital?'

'I've decided to take a chance and not be too cautious,' Vanessa answered. 'I've got some men coming to dig out hogweed at the week-end and a builder coming to put windows in the barn on Monday morning. Perhaps you could put me on to a good printer in town. I want to have some advertising posters done.'

'Oh dear! I do wish you'd talked things over with Ian first. He could have—'

'Why should I talk anything over with Ian?' Vanessa said sharply, then fearing she might have sounded rude, she added: 'I'm sorry, Freda, but I prefer to make my own decisions, then if I make mistakes I have only myself to blame.'

Freda was silent for a moment, then she said quietly: 'Neither Ian nor I have any desire to tell you what you should do, Vanessa, only to help.'

'Yes, I know,' Vanessa answered, feeling guilty. 'But I want to make my own way as far as possible, and in any case you *are* helping me.'

'Who is it who's coming to tackle the weed?' asked Freda.

'Some men Miles Kendal knows.'

'At time and a half?'

'Yes, I think so. But it will be worth it.' The other girl gave a shrug of her shoulders. 'Look, Freda, I know what you're thinking,' Vanessa said raggedly. 'You would have liked me to ask Ian, and Ian would have got his men to come over and put in a couple of days or so, but look what happened last time when I tried to pay them. I'd rather have it this way, honestly.'

They loaded the shooting-brake with garden sundries and plants, leaving some heavier articles to be delivered. A cup of coffee, a visit to the printer and one or two items of Freda's shopping took them to lunch-time. Freda suggested they ate at the White Horse where Ian had taken her the day she had visited the solicitor.

'Isn't that rather expensive?' she said.

'It's no more expensive than anywhere else,' Freda answered, 'and you do get a good meal. Besides—and I hope you won't mind—Ian said he might join us.'

Vanessa would have done anything rather than have lunch with Ian, but how could she say so without hurting Freda? And strictly speaking she had no great quarrel with Ian.

'Of course I don't mind. By the way, I saw Ian last night,' she added. 'Did he tell you?'

'No. No, he didn't,' Freda answered thoughtfully.

'I knew he was taking Cecile out to dinner. Were you at the same place?'

'Miles called to see me and we had a run out there,' Vanessa told her briefly.

Evidently Ian hadn't thought seeing her was worth mentioning. He was already in the White Horse restaurant when they entered the place. He greeted Vanessa formally, invited them to have a glass of sherry and began to ask Freda if she had managed to get various items of shopping for him. Freda chatted brightly—a little too brightly, Vanessa thought, as if she were covering up in an awkward situation.

'Wait until you hear Vanessa's plans,' she said after a minute or two. 'She's decided to launch out right away and not wait until her plants and things are ready for Christmas.'

'Oh, really? Well, let's go and order lunch and you can tell me all about it while we eat.'

They went to a table which Ian had reserved for them, and when they had ordered, Ian pressed Vanessa for more details. Now and then Freda eyed her brother anxiously as if anticipating his disapproval. Vanessa noticed this vaguely as she talked, and thought it most extraordinary. He listened quietly at first, his face impassive, but his eyes alert, then when she paused he asked her one or two questions. Vanessa thought fleetingly that she did not care whether he approved or not, yet could not help feeling pleased when he said:

'It all sounds pretty good to me. May I make a suggestion?'

'Of course.'

'Don't try to stock absolutely everything at first. Leave yourself a margin of capital. If somebody asks for an item you haven't got, just say you can get it— even if it means a special trip into town. That way, you not only find out what the popular demands are, and don't waste your money on stocking what there isn't much sale for, you also build up a good reputation for yourself.'

'That's a good idea,' she said. 'Thanks.'

He shot her a keen glance as if making sure she wasn't being sarcastic.

'Who are these men who are coming to tackle the hog-weed for you at the week-end?' he asked then.

'I—don't know their names,' she told him.

He looked puzzled and before Vanessa could enlarge, which somehow she felt reluctant to do, Freda intervened.

'It's some men Miles Kendal knows,' she said quietly, with again that look as if she feared his reaction. 'Vanessa didn't like to ask for our men because last time they wouldn't accept payment.'

'I daresay they'd have been willing to come at the usual rate if they'd been approached,' he said brusquely. 'There are limits to the number of times one can *offer* help.'

There was a heavy silence. An apology hovered on Vanessa's lips, but a look at Ian's granite-like face, and she asked herself what had she for which to apologize.

'Miles just happens to be around at the right time,' she said with a show of indifference.

'Which seems to be quite often.'

At this her lips tightened angrily. She lifted up her chin and sought for the right words with which to answer him. But he spoke first.

'I'm sorry. It's no business of mine who you spend your time with, of course.'

But his tone held neither regret nor concern. It had a strong hint of contempt.

'You're so right,' she was goaded into replying.

Freda looked frankly horrified. 'For goodness' sake, you two, stop snapping at each other!'

'I wasn't aware that I was snapping,' Ian answered coolly. 'I thought I had just offered an apology—and that for seeming to interfere in something which didn't concern me. Namely, the kind of friends Vanessa makes.'

'Well, you didn't *sound* very apologetic,' his sister retorted, 'and what you've just said only makes matters worse.'

Ian gave her a long look. 'There are several replies I could make to that, but I won't make any at all. Let's just eat.'

Vanessa ate without tasting anything, her mind occupied with various permutations of what replies Ian would have made to his sister's remark. But after a minute or two of silence, Freda said brightly:

'Vanessa is going to have the shooting-brake, Ian, so on the way home will you call at the garage and tell Bill I'll have that little runabout he was showing me the other day.'

He gave her another long look. 'Oh. Well, I'm very glad about that. You'll find the brake very useful, Vanessa. It's in good running order, but if you should have any troubles, let me know.'

'Thank you.' She decided she had better not start talking to him about the price. She would leave it to Freda to work out with him. She thought she was beginning to understand Ian. He was not only accustomed to having his own way, to being the boss, he was accustomed to women who were more pliant than she was. He liked to organize people, and he preferred women of the helpless female type—if they existed these days—rather than one like herself. Above all, it hurt his pride that another man, especially one whom he disliked as he did Miles, was being more helpful than he himself.

He did not stay for coffee. As soon as the sweet course had been served and eaten, he asked them to excuse him, and rose, paying the bill before he left.

'I ought to pay for my own lunch,' Vanessa protested.

'Don't be silly,' Freda said. 'I never knew anyone so independent.'

'I don't think I'm abnormally so. Anyhow, isn't it better than being a sponger?'

'Yes, I suppose it is, but both Ian and I *want* to help you.'

'I know, and I appreciate it. But Miles is anxious to be of help too. In fact, people are being extraordinarily kind, but I've been brought up to stand on my own feet as far as possible. I haven't *refused* help from anyone. It's just that I want to pay my own way.'

'Of course you do,' Freda said warmly. 'That's what I—' She broke off as if she had started to say something she shouldn't. 'But never mind. By the way, the Forestry Club meets next Wednesday. You will come, won't you?'

Vanessa said she'd love to. She had received a membership card and a programme and it looked very interesting. Freda drove back to Barn Hill and helped to unload the shooting-brake.

'I'll bring the brake round just as soon as I get the other car,' she promised as she was leaving.

By the week-end the barn had four large windows, and Vanessa had also made sure the builders had taken away the resultant rubble.

Vanessa eyed the inside walls ruefully. When the barn had had very little light, they had not looked so bad. Now they did not look so good.

'I'm afraid they'll have to be painted,' she said to Nancy.

Nancy smiled wickedly. 'Why don't you get Miles Kendal to do it? I'm sure he'll be glad to. Emulsion paint is what you want. With a large brush it will go on easily enough. It's too uneven to do with a roller.'

Vanessa took up the challenge. 'All right, Nancy, I will ask him. Perhaps Mr Watts will deliver the paint for me. I shall need quite a lot. Meanwhile I'll sweep a few spiders' webs away.'

The men came about ten o'clock and Vanessa had to admit they certainly could dig. Miles arrived just in time for coffee, but Vanessa had made a start on the painting herself, and was half way up a step-ladder.

'Good lord,' he exclaimed. 'What in the name of goodness are you doing?'

'What does it look like?'

'It looks like you're doing something you shouldn't.'

She hid a smile. 'Perhaps you wouldn't mind giving me a hand. I'm not doing right the way up to the ceiling, just taking a line from floor level to the tops of the windows.'

The white-painted bricks were going to look most attractive, but a second coat was going to be needed for a good clear finish. She popped the brush into a tin containing water and climbed down as Nancy called out that coffee was ready.

Miles gave her a helping hand and gazed all around, a frown on his face.

'It's going to take an age to cover all this. I know a good man who—'

'Sorry, Miles,' she cut in. 'I simply can't afford to pay for any more labour. If you don't want to help me, I shall just have to do it myself.'

'Don't be silly. Of course I want to help you. I don't like to see *you* doing these jobs, that's all.'

She gave his hand a squeeze. 'Thank you, Miles,' she said mischievously. 'I knew you would. Nancy—' she called out as they went out into the open. 'Isn't it wonderful? Miles is going to paint the barn for me.'

'Very wonderful,' agreed Nancy in a tone which said it was too good to be true.

Miles gave a large sigh. 'Well, it's not a job I'm too keen on, but for you I'd do practically anything.'

Later, when Miles was up the step-ladder applying paint to the wall, Vanessa whispered a triumphant ' I told you so ', in Nancy's ear. But Nancy sniffed.

' He isn't doing it for nothing, you mark my words.'

But suddenly the joke was over. ' As to that, Nancy, he hasn't any more an ulterior motive for being helpful than, say, Ian Hamilton. They've both got their eyes on Puck's Hill—or had. And in actual fact, Miles is being far more helpful in my business enterprise than either Ian or Freda. Don't get me wrong. I like Freda and she's being very friendly and helpful, but both she and Ian have discouraged me from launching out. If Miles still wanted me to sell Puck's Hill, he wouldn't be at all anxious for me to succeed in a business, would he? Quite the reverse.'

And having explained everything to her own satisfaction, at least, she found another paintbrush, opened a second tin of paint and started on the opposite wall from Miles. This way, using large brushes and not stinting the paint, the whole barn was covered by evening. And Vanessa was quite staggered at the amount of weed the two men had dealt with.

They left at five o'clock, promising to come the following day, and Vanessa invited Miles to stay for dinner.

' It's absolutely wonderful,' she exclaimed enthusiastically, surveying the large area of uprooted weed, after they had eaten. ' Miles, you're a genius!'

He grinned. ' Of course. Come over here and show me how much you appreciate me.'

Lounging on the roomy, old-fashioned settee, he held out his arm to her. She felt there was little else she could do, in all conscience, except go to him. She sat down beside him and his arm encircled her shoulders.

' I *do* appreciate all you've done, Miles,' she told him again. ' More than I can say. If we can do the same tomorrow, it will all be finished—at least most of it, and I shall be able to set out my " shop ".'

At the mention of tomorrow Miles sat up startled. ' Did you say the same tomorrow? I'm absolutely worn out after *today's* effort!'

She couldn't tell whether he was joking or not. She laughed lightly. ' Well, the men are coming tomorrow, anyway. And I've made up my mind to a week-end of work. A second coat of paint to the barn won't take long. Of course, I don't expect you to—'

He silenced her effectively by covering her lips with his. ' What are you talking about?' he murmured, kissing her again and yet again. ' If you want me to help you, of course I will.' He grinned sheepishly. ' Only trouble is, I'm likely to over-sleep on Sundays.'

He gave her a long, questioning look, a smile of amusement around his mouth. It was obvious that he was giving her a very strong hint to invite him to stay the night, and it seemed to her a very good idea. Why should he go back to an empty flat and have to fend for himself when he had worked so hard and would undoubtedly be coming again tomorrow?

' Well, there are plenty of spare bedrooms, and after all, I am chaperoned, so why not sleep here? That way, I can make sure you get up in good time in the morning,' she finished with a mischievous smile.

' You scheming little so'n'so,' he said, pulling her towards him. ' But I'll accept your offer with the greatest of pleasure.'

It was rather nice having Miles to stay the night. Vanessa realized how lonely she had been, in spite of having Nancy living with her. There was something very, very satisfying, she thought, in ' having a man about the house '.

Oddly enough, considering her hard day's work the previous day, Vanessa wakened fairly early on Sunday morning, and at about the time Nancy usually rose, Vanessa took her her breakfast upstairs.

' A Sunday morning treat for you, Nancy,' she said. ' And one you richly deserve.'

Nancy sat up and looked at the clock guiltily. ' Oh

133

dear! Thanks, Vanessa. But what got you up so early?'

She smiled. 'Got work on my mind, I expect.'

'What about your visitor? Not up yet?'

'Not a sound from him so far.'

'What are you going to do? Wait until he wakens?'

Vanessa considered for a moment. 'I think I'll open his door and take a peep in, then if he's respectable, go and shake him. If I don't, he's liable to sleep half the day away.'

Nancy tut-tutted. 'Well, at least you've saved me having to sit down to breakfast with him.'

A cup of tea in her hand, Vanessa pounded on Miles's door, but there was no response, so she opened it and looked in. Miles was still fast asleep, his head under the bedclothes. She put the cup of tea on the bedtable and gave him a good shake and removed the sheet from his face.

'Hey, Miles, wake up! It's ten o'clock and the sun's shining fit to burst. I've brought you a cup of tea.'

With a great deal of grunting and moaning he half opened his eyes and looked at her.

'Good lord, is it really you, or am I still dreaming?'

'It's really me. Drink that cup of tea and then rise and shine. Breakfast will be in ten minutes.'

When she went downstairs again, the labourers had already arrived. Vanessa cooked a breakfast of bacon and eggs and toast and she and Miles ate it in the kitchen. They were in the middle of the meal when suddenly Ian Hamilton walked in and stood in the open doorway.

CHAPTER VII

Ian looked at Miles in astonishment.

'You're here early, aren't you?'

Miles eyed him with amusement. 'I stayed the night, old boy. Any more questions?'

'No. I'm sorry I asked that one.' He turned to Vanessa, his face like stone. 'I've brought Freda's brake round for you. You can settle up with her when it suits you.'

He turned and walked out again. Vanessa pushed back her chair and ran to the door.

'Ian—' She caught him up and put a detaining hand on his arm. 'Ian, thank you.'

He gave her a look of contempt and deliberately removed her hand from his arm. What came over her, she didn't know, but it seemed imperative that he should understand.

'Ian, what's the matter? I only asked Miles to stay the night because he—'

But the scorn in his eyes still remained. 'You don't owe me any explanations, Vanessa. It's no concern of mine what you do, either now or at any other time.'

He strode off, and as she stood and watched him, Vanessa's anxiety to be understood and not judged wrongly turned to a consuming anger.

'If it wasn't for hurting Freda's feelings I'd fling the wretched shooting-brake back at him!' she declared to Miles when she stormed back into the kitchen.

'What's up?' he asked. 'Hamilton been his usual charming self?'

'Yes.' Vanessa took a deep breath.

'Sit down and I'll pour you another cup of coffee. How much are they asking for the brake, anyway?'

Miles poured out the coffee and sweetened it for her.

When Vanessa told him the figure Freda had mentioned he grimaced.

'Sounds like a bargain, but you can never tell. Anyway, if it's what you want, I should just ignore him—which is all he deserves—and accept it as from his sister. No use cutting off your nose to spite your face.'

'I suppose not.'

She was tremendously grateful for Miles throughout the whole of that Sunday. Ian's attitude niggled her all day, on and off, but Miles was charming, understanding and helpful. By the time evening came, there was not another piece of hogweed which was not uprooted and the interior walls of the barn had had their second coat of paint. Miles had even helped her to put up trestle tables on which to stand plants and other items and had carried in some of the heavier goods like bags of seeds and potting compost and various garden tools.

'Miles, I'm never going to be able to thank you enough,' she told him at the end of the day as they sat side by side on the settee with their after-dinner coffee.

'Darling girl, don't try,' he said softly. He put down his empty coffee cup and relieved her of hers, then took her in his arms. He kissed her, then flicked his gaze over her face, running his finger lightly down her straight nose. 'You know, I've learned quite a lot this weekend.'

'Really? How to paint a wall in two easy lessons?' she jested.

But he shook his head seriously. 'I know now what I've suspected for some time. I'm in love with you.'

She caught her breath and something within her contracted sharply. 'Miles! Oh—oh, Miles!'

Suddenly he crushed her to him. 'Darling girl, I want to marry you.'

Vanessa felt tears prick her eyes. 'Oh, Miles, I—I don't know what to say.'

'Why not just say yes?' He kissed the lobe of her ear and her smooth cheek.

It would be easy, so easy, she thought, in an odd sort of panic. This week-end with Miles in the house, the way they had worked together, had shown her how much she needed the companionship that only a happy marriage could give. And yet she hesitated.

'Miles, I'd rather—think about it for a little while, if you don't mind. You see, I'm—not sure.'

'I expect I've rushed you. You're so sweet. Anyway, you haven't said no, have you?'

'No, I haven't.'

'Bless you! It means a lot to me. More than you'll ever know.'

He kissed her again. 'We could be so happy together, you and I. I've never wanted anything so much in my whole life as to spend the rest of my days with you.'

Vanessa closed her eyes. The idea sounded wonderful, wonderful, except that, somehow there was the echo of a pain somewhere deep inside her. Later, when Miles had gone, she realized she was still affected by Ian Hamilton's visit of that morning.

Why did she let him bother her so much? she asked herself as she lay awake in bed. But of course, this must be the influence he had on everyone. This way he had of showing his disapproval, for instance. Its effect was that you wanted to please him, that you sought for his approval, that you were worried when you did not have it. Yes, that was it, she decided. And it was the same in the way he had of wanting to rule everyone's life. It made people defer to him. There was evidence of this in the way Freda looked to him and expected others to do so also. He made you feel you owed him something, that he had certain rights.

Impatient with herself, she turned over and tried to shut him out of her mind. She didn't care if she never saw him again.

Her posters arrived from the printers the following morning. Vanessa drove the shooting-brake into the village and called at the various shops asking them to display one for her. All promised to do so and wished her well. The butcher went a step further. As well as nailing one of them on a tree in a very prominent position outside his shop which would catch the eye of passing motorists, he asked for a second one to stick on his delivery van.

In the post office she met Freda, whose manner was noticeably cooler, but she managed to smile and say hello.

'Thanks for the brake—and for transferring the tax and insurance for me,' Vanessa said. 'It was very kind of you.'

'That's all right, though thanks are due to Ian, really. He attended to everything.'

Vanessa sighed. 'I tried to thank Ian yesterday morning when he brought the brake round, but he didn't seem to want my thanks—or anything else.'

A worried look settled on Freda's face. 'Well, it's rather difficult for Ian. You know how he feels about Miles Kendal—and he has good reason. It isn't just uncharitableness. He—didn't expect to find Miles having breakfast with you.'

'But there was nothing wrong in that!' Vanessa protested warmly. 'Miles was tired. He'd been painting the interior of the barn for me all day, and he was coming the following day too, so I asked him to stay the night, that's all. I'm afraid I can't choose my friends just to please Ian.'

'He doesn't expect you to,' Freda answered quietly. 'It's just that he's—concerned about you. He knows Miles Kendal far better than you do. Almost certain to.'

'But—but why should he be so concerned?' demanded Vanessa exasperatedly.

Freda looked rather disconcerted. 'Well, for one

138

thing, because of knowing your aunt, I suppose. For another, we're neighbours and—I hope—friends. And apart from that, I think Ian would be concerned for any woman he knew under similar circumstances.'

Vanessa still thought he had a highly exaggerated sense of responsibility which in effect meant that he liked to dominate. But she liked Freda and did not want to lose her friendship, if it could be avoided. So she said, without a great deal of conviction:

' I think I understand, but one can only take people as one finds them, and Miles has been a help.'

But the troubled look did not leave Freda's face. ' Is it true you're going to marry him, Vanessa?' she asked.

Vanessa looked at her in astonishment. ' How could you possibly know anything about that? He only asked me last night.'

' Then it's true?'

' I haven't made up my mind yet. But how—'

Freda evaded the unspoken and the spoken question. ' Look, Vanessa, I must fly. Shall we see you at the Foresters' Club meeting next week?'

' Yes, I think so.'

' Good. See you then.'

She hurried away. Vanessa looked after her with a sigh. If only she and Ian were not so dead set against Miles. People could be business rivals without disliking each other, surely?

During the ensuing week, Miles called to see her every day. Sometimes, not until late evening, at others during the day. On the Monday evening he brought her flowers, and when he took her in his arms, he asked:

' Made up your mind yet, darling?'

She shook her head and gave an apologetic smile. ' I've been too busy to think about it very much. I'm sorry.'

He kissed her. ' Not to worry. And I won't keep on badgering you. It isn't " no ", anyway, is it?'

She shook her head.

'Well, that's something.'

It wasn't until he had gone that she remembered what Freda had said in the post office. She had intended asking Miles how it had come about that Ian and Freda knew he had asked her to marry him. But she became so busy with her new business, the matter went out of her head except at the wrong times.

She had a very good response to her posters. Some of the people, she suspected, came more out of curiosity, but they strolled around that part of the garden which was already cultivated, had a pot of tea and some of Nancy's home-made cakes, browsed among the plants and other goods, and in the majority of cases ended up by buying either a pot plant or something for the garden. When she was not busy attending to customers, she helped Joe to heap the uprooted giant hogweed in one place for burning. The next step would be to hire a bulldozer to level the ground ready for the laying of turf.

She saw nothing of Ian Hamilton at all, and when Freda dropped in one evening, she did not even mention his name. Perversely, Vanessa itched to ask about him, but it somehow did not occur to her to ask simply: 'How is Ian?'

Miles said he would like to go to the meeting of the Foresters' Club, and as members were allowed to take a guest, Vanessa naturally invited him to be hers. He called for her on the night, but before they set out he put his arm about her and produced a small box from his pocket. It contained an engagement ring.

'Like it?' he asked, opening the box to show it to her.

'It's—beautiful, Miles. Really beautiful,' she told him rather worriedly, as the big diamond solitaire ring set in platinum winked up at her.

'Are you going to let me put it on for you?'

She shook her head swiftly. 'No—please, Miles. Not yet. I—I think I'd rather get this business of mine going before I think of getting married.'

He smiled. 'Darling girl, I'm not suggesting you should pack it in. You can still carry on with that if you want to. I'd be quite willing to move in here with you. I can soon let my flat. What do you say?'

She wanted to say yes. Miles had shown her without any shadow of doubt that he loved her, and the warmth of feeling she had for him was equal to anything she had felt for any man. Yet somehow she felt she still wanted more time.

'Miles, I'm reasonably sure. But give me to the end of the week, will you? Come to lunch on Sunday and we'll talk about it then.'

'Talk about it? All I want is one word.'

'I know. The—the truth is, Miles, I—had one disappointing affair just before I came here and I suppose it's made me cautious. I don't seem to be able to trust my own feelings—or even know what they are. Maybe it's too soon on top of the other.'

He hugged her. 'All right, darling girl, I understand. Take all the time you want. I'd rather that than rush you into saying no.'

She hardly knew what to say. His caring was touching her deeply, and she knew that fundamentally, this was what she needed. To be cared for, to be loved, not merely 'helped'. Her need went deeper than ordinary friendship. Almost she said yes to Miles then and there, but she contented herself with putting her arms around his neck and kissing his cheek.

'Hey, that's no use,' he said, and covered her lips with his. Then when he released her: 'Tell you what, darling girl. Pop the ring into your bag, then when you're sure, just put it on your finger. I'll keep a sharp look-out for it, believe me!'

He dropped the little box into her handbag.

They were just going out of the door when the telephone rang. Vanessa turned back.

'I'd better answer it. It might be for me, and I think Nancy's upstairs.'

She lifted the receiver to find Freda at the other end. 'I was wondering whether we could go to the Club together,' she said. 'There's no point in taking two cars if one will do, is there?'

'That's—very kind of you, Freda, but Miles is coming as my guest and he has his car, so I shall be coming with him.'

'Oh. Oh, I see,' Freda answered in a flat voice. 'All right, Vanessa. See you there.'

Obviously having heard her side of the short conversation, Miles's face held the smile of amusement he seemed always to reserve for whenever Freda or Ian were mentioned. Vanessa felt suddenly irritated.

'What's funny, Miles?' she asked sharply.

He laughed. 'Darling girl, it *is* funny. Don't you see? He's so accustomed to being top dog. He's been trying to be the great friend and protector, the man to whom everyone—and especially yourself—turns to for help and advice, the man every woman worships and looks up to and so on *ad nauseam*. You have shown him that you want none of it—or of him. And the fact that another man is having some measure of success where he is failing must be burning him up. The more so as *I* happen to be the man. I should think he's fairly gnashing his teeth.'

But Vanessa still did not think it was funny, even though Miles's description of Ian fitted in with her own opinion of him. She felt Ian was far too dignified to be 'gnashing his teeth', as Miles put it. He might have a strong sense of pride, but she felt sure Ian would never be guilty of petty jealousy.

Miles's attitude to Ian and Ian's dislike of Miles niggled her all the way to the Foresters' Club room. But Miles was in excellent spirits, not only during the short journey, but in the Club room, so much so that Vanessa found herself becoming increasingly irritated and discomfited. He was not like the same person in the company of others. He was more brash, more possessive than she liked, acting as though he had already proprietorial rights over her, constantly putting his arm around her shoulders, calling her 'darling', hardly leaving her side for a moment, until at last she managed to get away from him to cross the room to speak to Freda.

'Hello, Vanessa,' Freda said quietly, giving her a long look. 'Miles is creating a certain impression. Does he have grounds?'

Vanessa frowned. 'No, not really. I—don't know what's come over him. He's so different when we're alone together.'

'The one you're seeing now is the one we know—Ian and I. And I think the same goes for most people.'

'Perhaps you don't know him sufficiently well,' Vanessa said. 'People often behave differently in a crowd. Not everyone's reactions are the same.' She glanced around the room. 'Is—Ian coming tonight?'

'Later, I hope. Though in a way, it might be better if he stays away.'

'Why?' asked Vanessa. She simply could not believe that either Miles's behaviour or her own would have all that much influence on him.

But Freda was looking towards the door. 'Here comes Ian now anyway.'

She waved to him and he joined them immediately. As he strode across the room, distinguished-looking in his fine tweeds, Vanessa felt something inside her contract painfully. He nodded to them gravely and said in a quiet voice:

'Good evening, Vanessa. Glad you made it. Did you come with Freda?'

Vanessa was about to answer. Why should she be afraid to say she had come with Miles? But Freda inter-

143

vened swiftly.

'Excuse me, both of you. It's my turn to help with coffee tonight. Ian, why don't you and Vanessa go and sit over there—' she indicated a corner half hidden by a stack of spare chairs. 'I'll bring you both a cup of coffee.'

Ian looked enquiringly at Vanessa. She nodded, and he put his hand under her elbow and led her between the groups of people standing talking to each other.

'It's—a long time since we've seen each other, Vanessa,' Ian said when they were seated. 'How's the business going? I've seen your posters around.'

She had the feeling that he was merely being polite, and wished Freda had not manoeuvred them into this corner together. But she answered that it was going well and then found herself warming up to the subject.

'You haven't seen the barn since I've had windows put in, have you?'

'No, I haven't.'

'Oh, then you must,' she said, forgetting in her enthusiasm that the last time Ian and herself had met they had almost quarrelled. 'It looks marvellous. The walls are painted white and they make a perfect background for plants. I shall have to think about some heating before the winter comes, of course, and it won't be long before I shall need another greenhouse.'

His face relaxed into a smile. 'You'll soon be needing an assistant too, by the sound of things. Your aunt would have been proud of you. But how are things going financially—if you don't mind my asking.'

'Of course I don't mind,' she told him warmly, aware of an extraordinary feeling of lightness, their differences forgotten. 'I'm not quite at the end of the money Aunt Maud left for me, but I don't think I shall have very much in hand by the time I've paid for the levelling of the ground and the turfing. Still, I hope to start showing a profit in a few weeks' time.'

'Have you got much ground clearance to do yet?' he asked.

'No, not a lot,' she told him. 'The hogweed is nearly all stacked now ready for burning, so—'

'Have you contacted a firm to do the levelling?' he queried.

She shook her head. 'Not yet. Do you know of one?'

'Better than that. I've got a plant you can borrow— or hire, if you insist. Although strictly speaking I ought not to hire it to you as I'm not in the plant hire business. But if you really want to pay something, pay the man who operates it the basic rate for the job.'

It was a relief to be able to say yes to his offer. Freda appeared with their coffee and looked swiftly from one to the other.

'Well, you two look happy enough, anyhow, and if I were you I'd stay right there.'

Vanessa smiled contentedly. She felt as though she could go on sitting here talking to Ian indefinitely. Something odd was happening to her. She had rarely felt so at peace. As Freda went off again, she caught Ian's eye and smiled, feeling extraordinarily shy.

'Have you done anything about those piano or guitar lessons?' Ian asked her after a moment or two.

'No, I haven't. But I intend to,' she told him with sudden decision. 'Somehow I haven't felt like it, and with my new business and all I—haven't had a minute. But now I shall.'

Music seemed suddenly an essential part of her life, and she felt so light-hearted she wanted to laugh out loud.

'Do you pick up new things quickly?' he asked.

'I think so, and once I start on anything I usually stick to it and want to reach a certain standard.'

'Yes, I can imagine you would.' He smiled. 'We'll forget about the guitar. There is *one* difficulty you'll find when you come to learn to play the piano. Your fingers will be stiff for a while. Even those who can play well find the same if they haven't touched the piano for some time. So you'd have to be content with very little more than five-finger exercises for a week or two.'

More and more people had come into the Club room since Freda and Vanessa had arrived and now Vanessa and Ian were hemmed in almost completely. But Ian was leaning slightly to one side and looking across the room. He frowned, then shot an enquiring look at Vanessa.

'Kendal is looking for someone. Could it be you?'

'Possibly.'

'Then don't let me keep you.'

He half rose from his seat, but Vanessa shook her head swiftly.

'No, no, please. I—I'd rather stay here and—and talk to you for a little while longer.'

His eyes widened, then his brows contracted in a puzzled frown and his expression became guarded.

'There was a rumour going around that you and he were engaged.'

She shook her head slowly. 'He asked me, but I—haven't made up my mind yet.'

'Why not?'

She stared at him, not knowing quite how to take the query. She would have expected him to show disapproval that she had not turned Miles down completely, instead of which his tone hinted that she ought to have accepted him.

She tried to answer Ian, but it was not easy to frame the right words.

'Well, I—I don't think I want to get married yet. I've only just started on my business project, and—'

'Don't "feelings" come into it?'

'Feelings?' she echoed, as if she had never heard of the word.

146

'Yes, feelings,' he repeated. 'Are you in love with the man or aren't you?'

She felt her cheeks warming. 'I—don't think you have any right to ask me such personal questions. But if it's of any great interest to you, I—I'm not sure. I don't know whether I trust love, anyway.'

The ghost of a smile played around his mouth. 'Disillusioned at your age?'

'One can be disillusioned at any age,' she retorted.

'True, but one doesn't usually associate disillusion with love in someone as young and—shall we say as attractive as you.'

Her eyes widened at the compliment, but she reminded him: 'I didn't say I *was* disillusioned. That was your word. It just happens that—experience has taught me to be cautious, that's all.'

'Experience?' He caught up the word as if to examine and analyse it. Then he said: 'I'm sorry. Sorry that you should have had that kind of experience.'

She smiled faintly. 'It's all a part of life, I suppose.'

'Well, you've recovered sufficiently to be able to be philosophical about it, evidently. But it has still left you cautious.'

'Every experience leaves its mark, I suppose. And in the case of—disappointment in love, one tends to mistrust one's emotions,' she answered.

He gave her a long look. 'If you were really and truly in love, you wouldn't be thinking this way—trying to analyse your feelings.'

'You think not? Perhaps one learns to control one's emotions as well as to mistrust them. And maybe I'm not a very emotional or—ardent kind of person.'

His eyes narrowed in a calculating look. 'I would stake my life on it that you are. If you've never felt really passionately in love, then I would say you've never *been* in love. No man has been successful in rousing these feelings in you yet, that's all.'

She opened her eyes wide. She didn't know whether to laugh or be indignant.

' And what gives you such wonderful insight as to the kind of person I am?' she demanded.

' Well, you're not exactly placid. And you've shown that you're capable of a great warmth of affection from the way you came to nurse your aunt. Added to that you're something of a spitfire, aren't you?'

' Am I?'

' You are indeed.'

Vanessa could hardly believe that they were talking like this. The jumbled sound of voices in varying tones, bursts of laughter, the chink of glasses or cups and saucers broke over their heads, but they were in a world apart. A man and a woman talking, getting close to each other, finding out about each other. Vanessa felt a strange sense of unreality, as if she and Ian were standing high on a mountain top, their hands clasped, their fingers entwined. It was important. Treasure this time, hold on to it.

She gave a little smile. ' You've been analysing me. What about you? *I've* been hearing rumours, as well.'

He thought for a moment. ' I daresay you have. But tell me what you've heard.'

But now Vanessa felt alone on the mountain top. She had asked the wrong question. She had wanted to find out what kind of man *he* was, how he would treat a woman, whether indeed he would be ardent. Instead, mentioning rumours about him had only served to remind her of Cecile Harland and even to talking about her.

' Well, I—heard that you were once in love with Miss Harland, that you—only came to Barn Hill because of her.'

He raised his eyebrows. ' Is that all?'

' Briefly, yes. It—tells its own story, surely. Is it

148

true?'

'Partly. I did know Cecile before Freda and I moved to this part of the country, but of course there were other reasons why we came here.'

Other reasons. So Cecile *had* been one of them? And was he still in love with her? It was a question she could not ask him, naturally, and she would not have wanted to. She asked herself why, and knew that it was because she would dread the answer. She did not want him still to be in love with Cecile. She did not want him to be in love with anyone. She stared into her empty coffee cup, aware that it was her turn to speak, yet not knowing quite what to say. There were so many things she wanted to know about him, but it was impossible to ask. She became aware, too, of his scrutiny, and when she raised her eyes to look at him, she knew she was in love with him.

'Do you ever wonder,' he asked, changing the subject, 'what the conditions of your aunt's will are?'

She shook her head dazedly. What did Aunt Maud's will matter? What did anything matter except that she was here and Ian was here and she loved him?

'No, I—haven't even thought about it,' she answered a trifle breathlessly.

'That's very strange. Most people would have tried to hazard a guess or two.'

'I've had so many other things on my mind. And if I did try to guess, what good would it do? I would have no idea whether my guesses were right or wrong.'

'No,' he agreed. 'On the other hand, it might help if you were to give the matter some thought. I believe you said there was a considerable sum of money involved. One of the conditions of inheritance might be that you shouldn't marry. How would you feel about that?'

She stared at him. 'Surely Aunt Maud wouldn't make any such condition?'

149

'She might. She never married herself, and she might not like the idea of a man invading her house and property.'

'All she asked,' she said after a moment's thought, 'was that I shouldn't sell Puck's Hill. The other part of the will only concerns money.'

'Which you might not get if you marry.'

Vanessa eyed him uncertainly. 'You—think I should remain forever single—never marry?'

'That's for you to decide, isn't it?' he countered.

'Decision is not the word I would use,' she answered, her eyes flicking over his tanned features, wondering fleetingly how long she had loved him, really. 'What is money? When one falls in love deeply, marriage is the natural, the only thing.'

His gaze was on her face too, and once more they were together on the mountain top.

'So you would give up everything for the man you loved?'

'Of course.'

'You really are worth wooing and pursuing, Vanessa,' he said in an oddly quiet voice.

Her heartbeat quickened, and the hand holding her cup and saucer trembled. Then someone jogged her elbow and her cup fell sideways, spilling the dregs on her dress. At once there were apologies, people turning to look at them, and someone took the cup from her hand. The magic moments were over. Vanessa opened her bag to get out a handkerchief to mop her dress, but when she pulled it out, the ring case came with it and dropped on the floor. The lid was evidently not on properly. It flew open at Ian's feet, revealing the ring in all its significant sparkle.

He picked it up and handed it back to her, his face a mask, his eyes cold.

'Yours, I believe,' he said icily, and walked away into the crowd.

CHAPTER VIII

Miles was at her elbow now. ' Darling, so here you are. I've been looking everywhere for you.'

Vanessa stood up and looked vaguely around, trying to see where Ian had gone, wanting to hurry after him to explain. He thought she had lied to him, that she *was* engaged to Miles. How could she make him understand?

She became aware of Miles's scrutiny. ' What's the matter, Vanessa—and how did you come to be pinned in this corner with Hamilton? Has he been annoying you?'

She shook her head swiftly. ' No, no, of course not. But I think I'd like to go home, if you don't mind.'

' Go home?' he echoed. ' But the evening's only half over.'

She wished she had brought her own car. It was unfair to drag Miles away really, but she felt she must get away. Miles drew her into the centre of the room, his hand under her elbow, but there were only two things in Vanessa's mind—Ian, and Miles's ring, once more in her handbag. Where was he? Was there someone else who would give her a lift home. She saw Freda collecting coffee cups, a worried look on her face. Vanessa caught her eye, and Freda carried her tray into the kitchen, then came across the room.

' What happened in the corner there, Vanessa? Ian's gone out looking furious.'

Miles put his arm across Vanessa's shoulders. ' Your brother looks furious at the drop of a hat. It's my guess that Vanessa is the one who should be looking furious, but like the sweet girl she is, she's probably apportioning all the blame for any—misunderstanding to herself. Come along, Vanessa, I'll take you home.'

Vanessa looked apologetically at Freda. 'Perhaps we can get together and talk one day. I really must get home. Goodnight, Freda.'

She was glad that Miles did not talk much on the way to Barn Hill. When they arrived at the house he held out his hand.

'Give me your key, Vanessa. I'll unlock the door for you.'

Without protest she gave it to him and when he had unlocked the door, he followed her inside. She invited him into the library. There were things she must say to him.

'Would you like some coffee?' she asked, trying to collect her thoughts together.

He shook his head. 'I've already had two cups. Come and sit down and tell me what's upset you. One of these days I'll kill Hamilton!'

He took her hand and made her sit down, dropping on to the settee beside her. She withdrew her hand from his and took out the ring in its case.

'You'd better have this, Miles. I'm sorry—it has to be no, after all.'

He looked from the box to her in astonishment.

'But—but, darling girl, I don't understand. Less than a couple of hours ago you said you were reasonably sure, that you were going to tell me by the end of the week. What's happened to change things? I can't think that you've let Ian Hamilton poison your mind against me. Though it would be just like him to try.'

'No, no, it's nothing like that. Please, Miles. I—I'm sorry, but I can't marry you. I know it now for certain.'

'But—' he took both her hands in his. 'But how can you? It's not possible! I'm the same person that I was about an hour and a half ago, you're the same, so—'

She was not the same. She was different. Something had happened to her. She was a woman in love.

'Miles, you'll have to take my word for it. Please don't

prolong the argument. In fact, I don't want an argument at all. I told you I wasn't sure. Now I am. I'm not in love with you, Miles, that's all.'

He drew an angry breath. 'What's Hamilton been saying to you? It's got something to do with him, I know.'

Vanessa sighed and rose. 'Please, Miles, there's no point in discussing it. I'm sorry, truly I am, but liking isn't love, and these things often come to one suddenly.' She smiled and held out her hand to him. 'Good night, Miles, and thanks for seeing me home. Thanks for all you've done to help me, too.'

He eyed her keenly and stood up, ignoring her hand. 'All right, Vanessa. But I still think there's more in this than meets the eye. Believe me, Hamilton knows more about your affairs than you think. I wouldn't trust him an inch, if I were you. And for heaven's sake, don't fall in love with him. If you ever did, you'd live to rue it!'

He went out, obviously very hurt and angry, and she could not blame him, but what would have been the use of keeping him in doubt?

Ian. Oh, Ian!

She made her way slowly upstairs, loving him with every breath and with every step, yet wanting to weep at the memory of that cold look in his eyes when he handed Miles's ring back to her. She must see him, make him understand.

Scarcely aware of what she was doing, she made her preparations for bed, even though it was still quite early, her mind going over and over again everything they had talked about, everything he had said, the way he had looked, the tone of his voice—everything about him. She had loved him for a very long time, of course. That day at his house when she had been sitting on the edge of the pool, the night of the Foresters' dance when he had been dancing with Cecile Harland. She had been in

153

love with him then. Why hadn't she realized it before?

But now the thought of Ian and Cecile Harland filled her mind. Ian had not told her what she most wanted to hear—that though he had once been in love with Cecile, he was no longer.

Trying to sleep, Vanessa tossed about to the accompaniment of her thoughts in which questions and speculations bounced from one side of her brain to the other, but the most important questions were hurled back unanswered.

'You were home early last night,' Nancy commented the next morning, giving her a speculative look.

Vanessa nodded. 'I—wasn't enjoying the meeting very much, so I got Miles to run me home, then I went straight up to bed.'

'Was Ian at the meeting?' Nancy queried.

Vanessa sighed. 'Yes, he was.'

Nancy made no further comment about Ian. She observed: 'Miles Kendal didn't stay long, anyway, did he? I heard him drive away again quite soon after you came in.'

'That's right—and I don't suppose I shall be seeing so much of him in the future. I gave him back his ring last night.'

'I didn't know you'd ever accepted one from him,' Nancy said in a surprised voice.

Vanessa explained, 'It was silly, really. He dropped it into my bag, and I was to put it on when I decided I wanted to be engaged to him.'

'What made you make up your mind?' Nancy asked curiously. 'Something happen at the meeting?'

'You could say that, I suppose,' Vanessa answered briefly.

'Well, I can't say I'm sorry you've sent that young man packing,' Nancy said frankly. 'I'm sure you're well rid of him.'

But Vanessa did not think she *was* rid of him, as

Nancy put it. A few days later he called to see her.

'I came to apologize for my attitude when you gave me the ring back,' he said. 'I'm afraid I never was a very good loser.'

'I understand, Miles. I think I would have felt the same in your place. It's hard to accept defeat sometimes—if defeat is the right word.'

'It's the right word sure enough. But I came to ask if we could still be friends.'

'Why, yes, of course,' she said swiftly, anxious to make amends for having hurt him.

He smiled and put his arm across her shoulders. 'That's the girl! Well, come and see me off. I can't stay long this time. I've got someone to see down at the Swan.'

His arm still across her shoulder, they went outside and stood for a moment beside his car. Vanessa wished he would take his arm away, but it would seem unnecessarily unfriendly to shake it off, and he would soon be gone. But as they stood beside his car, another drove up. Vanessa needed only one glance to see that it was Ian. She shrugged her shoulders to remove Miles's arm, but he gripped them the more tightly. Ian got out of the car, looked from one to the other quickly, then stepped back in again and drove off without a word.

Miles threw back his head and laughed out loud. Vanessa rounded on him furiously.

'I don't think it's the least little bit funny,' she stormed. 'You deliberately kept your arm round my shoulder just to make him think the worst!'

'The worst? What on earth is that supposed to be? You care too much what Hamilton thinks.' He opened the door of his car. 'I understand that you and he were in quite a huddle in that corner the other night. I hope he didn't give you any wrong impressions. He likes to think he's keeping women on tenterhooks. I know quite a few who'd like to know where they stand with him.

But they're fools. He's got his eye on the main chance —and that means Cecile.'

He smiled and with an imperturbable wave, drove off down the drive.

Her eyes misty with tears, Vanessa felt for a moment as if she hated him. But all he had said about Ian could be the truth. He had talked to her last night as if he were genuinely interested in her as a woman, yet he had carefully evaded telling her what his relationship with Cecile was now. There was no real reason why he should have, of course, except that they *had* been talking on a personal level.

Between attending to the wants of customers and giving attention to her seedling plants Vanessa toyed with the idea of ringing Ian to find out why he had come. He must have wanted to see her about something. She hoped he would ring her, but he didn't. At last, one evening a few days later, she picked up the telephone and dialled his number. Again, it was Cecile who answered, and Vanessa was beginning to wonder whether she was living there.

' May I speak to Ian?' she asked determinedly. 'This is Vanessa Woodrow here.'

' Ian?' came the cool voice. ' Hang on a moment.'

Vanessa hung on, her heart beating swiftly, but it was Freda who answered after a minute or two and she did not say whether Ian was at home or not. Vanessa had to conclude, with despair, in her heart, that he simply did not want to speak to her.

' Oh, Vanessa,' said Freda, ' I'm coming along to see you in the morning. Will that be all right?'

' Yes, perfectly. Come and have coffee with me. I'd like to see you. But I wanted to speak to Ian. Is he—'

' I'm sorry, Vanessa,' came the answer. ' This is a bad line. I'll see you in the morning around eleven. 'Bye for now.'

Vanessa had no option but to hang up. She replaced

the receiver slowly, convinced that Ian had been there but did not want to speak to her. He thought her a person who lied, he felt a contempt for her because of her association with Miles. But she hadn't lied, and what was wrong with Miles anyway? She was rapidly coming to the conclusion afresh that Ian did not really like her and never had.

'Sorry I haven't been round before,' Freda said brightly when she arrived the following morning, 'but I don't seem to have had time to breathe. How are things with you? Business flourishing?'

Vanessa said it was and poured out coffee in her study/library. Freda glanced around at the walls, now painted in creamy white, the dusty books sold to an antiquarian book dealer.

'I say, this is marvellous. I haven't been in here since you've done it up,' she exclaimed, determined it seemed to Vanessa, to keep on talking trivialities.

'Ian called a day or so ago,' she said at last. 'Did he want to see me about something?'

'Er—yes. That's why I've come really. He asked me to. It was to tell you that his offer of a bulldozer to level the land still held good and you're to say what day you'd like the man to come. He also asked me to give you this.' She took a business card out of her bag and handed it to Vanessa. 'It's a firm of heating engineers—a friend of ours. Give him a ring and he'll come and discuss your greenhouse heating problems. The house too, if you want it. And if I were you, I *would* let him do the house. You can always regulate the amount you use, can't you?'

Vanessa swallowed hard and nodded, but at the moment the heating of either house or greenhouse, and the levelling of the land were of little interest to her. It was Ian she wanted to know about, to talk about.

'Did—Ian say anything after he'd called to see me

that day?'

From Freda's expression it was apparent that he had, but she hesitated before answering.

' Well, he did say that Miles Kendal was with you.'

' Is that all?'

' What else should there be?' asked Freda, giving her a steady look.

Vanessa pressed her hands to her face. ' I don't *know*—'

Freda's hand touched her arm. ' Vanessa, what's the matter? What happened between you and Ian the other evening at the club? He won't tell me anything, but he's certainly cut up about something.'

' He—thinks me a liar, I suppose. We—we were getting along quite well. At least, I thought we were until—'

' I thought you were too. What were you talking about?'

' Oh, all kinds of things. He—asked me if I was engaged to Miles, but I told him I hadn't made up my mind. He even asked me if I was in love with Miles, and I told him I wasn't sure about that either. We talked some more, then I—spilt some of my coffee on to my dress. I reached in my bag for my handkerchief to mop it up, and when I pulled it out, the ring box Miles had given me fell out. The—the top couldn't have been on properly. The ring fell out and—Ian picked it up. He didn't wait for me to explain. He just gave it back to me and walked away.'

Freda gave a puzzled frown. ' I don't quite understand, either. If you're not engaged to Miles, why did you have his ring in your bag?'

' He brought it with him when he called for me. I hadn't said I *would* marry him. He—he just brought it. But I still didn't want to accept it. I told him I'd give him a definite answer by the end of the week, so he said—" Well, put it in your bag, and when you've made up your mind to say yes, just put it on ".'

'I see. So I suppose Ian jumped to the conclusion you *were* engaged, seeing you were carrying Miles's ring around. Then he called the other day, and here Miles was again. You can hardly blame him, Vanessa, can you?'

'I suppose not. But why should he think I would lie? Does he think I'm that sort of person?'

Freda sighed. 'We all get a bit mixed up at times, Vanessa, and jump to wrong conclusions. And with regard to Miles Kendal, you've had me foxed at times, too. You didn't seem to be his type at all, and yet you've become so friendly with him. He always seems to be around, he's stayed the night here, you've accepted his help in preference to ours, and even now we don't know whether you're going to marry him or not.'

'I'm not,' Vanessa told her quietly.

Freda's delight at this news showed in her face. 'Oh, Vanessa, I'm so glad. So you've given him back his ring?'

Vanessa nodded. 'He was a bit annoyed at first, then he came the other day to apologize and ask if we could remain friends. I had to say yes, of course. We had no quarrel and he really has been a good friend. I'm only sorry that Ian happened to call just when he did. I was rather annoyed with Miles, actually. He stood with his arm round my shoulders and wouldn't move it even when Ian drove up.'

'Ah, so that was it.'

'That was what, exactly?' queried Vanessa.

'Well, it explains why Ian didn't stay and why he thought you and Miles——'

'I suppose so,' Vanessa said miserably. 'But I rang Ian yesterday to try to explain and he wouldn't even speak to me. He *was* at home, wasn't he, Freda? Because Cecile was there.'

Freda sighed worriedly. 'This is all very difficult,

Vanessa, and I hardly know what to say to you. Would you like me to explain things to Ian?'

Vanessa nodded, tears not far away. Explaining to Ian, making him believe that she had not lied to him about Miles would not alter the fact that he did not care for her, nor lessen her love for him, still less would it make Cecile cease to exist.

Freda eyed her closely. 'Why does it matter so much what Ian thinks, Vanessa? And what made you decide you didn't want to marry Miles?'

Vanessa's lips trembled. 'I can't tell you that, Freda.'

'I think I can guess,' Freda said softly.

With an effort Vanessa kept back her tears. 'If only he didn't dislike me so!'

'But, Vanessa, he doesn't dislike you.' She sighed again and stood up. 'Look, I must go now. There are a whole heap of things which need clearing up between you and Ian, but I can't very well speak for him. I'll tell him you really aren't engaged to Miles, anyway. I should think he'll be very pleased about that —for your sake. And what shall I tell him about the bulldozer?' she added swiftly.

The bulldozer. As if it mattered! The words which had held her attention were *for your sake*. If only it had been for his sake, too.

'The bulldozer can come any time at all,' she answered heavily. 'And thank Ian for me, of course.'

'I will.' Freda looked as though she were about to say something else, but changed her mind and took her leave.

Vanessa had longed to ask her about Cecile, but what would have been the use? she asked herself. She was sure the answer would have only added to the ache already in her heart.

She wondered whether Ian would ring her or call to see her after Freda had explained to him about the ring,

and during the following days her ear was continually
tuned to the telephone, her heart leaping every time it
rang. But there was nothing from him. The bulldozer
arrived and did a wonderful job of levelling the ground
where the weed had been dug out. Ian had received
her message about that obviously, then surely Freda had
given him the other? Vanessa shrank from dialling
their number. She did not want to risk Cecile answering
it again. As it was, in casting a look across the boundary fence she caught a glimpse of both Cecile and Ian
through the trees and turned quickly away. On another
occasion she saw Ian alone. She hesitated, then waved
and would have walked towards the boundary to speak
to him, but he turned away and she had no way of
knowing whether he had seen her or not. But she had
an awful feeling that he had and was deliberately avoiding her. Freda appeared to be avoiding her too. A
week passed and Vanessa saw nothing of her. When
she did, it was by accident in the village.

'I thought I might have seen you before, Freda,'
Vanessa said. 'Not knowing how I stand with Ian, I
didn't feel I could ring you or call at the house. You—
did tell Ian about everything?'

'Yes, Vanessa, I did.'

'What did he say?'

'He—said he was glad to hear it—that you weren't
engaged to Miles.'

'Is that all?'

'Well, yes. At least, that's all I can tell you, Vanessa.
I don't think he had really believed you capable of telling lies. He said he hadn't known what to think.'
Then she asked, in a way which Vanessa was sure was
aimed deliberately at changing the subject: 'Have you
been in touch with the heating engineer yet?'

Vanessa said she hadn't. She had had too many other
things on her mind.

'Do you intend to?'

'Oh yes, I must—even if it's only for the sake of my plants.'

Freda seemed once more in a hurry. 'I'll give you a ring, Vanessa, and you must come and have a meal with us again.'

But Vanessa felt as though she were being let down lightly, that neither Freda nor Ian were anxious to see her again.

On the same day that her turf was delivered the heating engineer called. He said he had been asked to by Ian.

'Only to advise you,' he said. 'You won't be under any obligation.'

'That's very good of you. It's my greenhouse I'm most concerned about, and the barn.'

'And what about the house? I understand you haven't any form of central heating there.'

'That's true, but I have a financial problem, Mr—'

'Hunt. Geoffrey Hunt. A good many people have financial problems, Miss Woodrow, but I think you'll find that what I have to suggest will be well within your means. But let me take a look around.'

She showed him the barn and greenhouse, then took him into the house. As soon as he saw that there was a fireplace in the hall he was delighted.

'Ah, Ian said he thought there was a fireplace. That solves the problem.'

'How?'

He explained that he could fix an oil heater there which would heat the entire house.

'No pipes or ducts are needed. Only one small pipe —and that would be to feed in the oil from a tank outside.'

'But how can one oil heater keep the whole house warm—and why must it be in the fireplace?'

'It works by ordinary convection currents,' he told her. 'And it must have a sixteen-foot-long flue pipe to carry away fumes. That's where the chimney comes in useful. The heat is sent out from the unit with such a force it permeates the whole house, especially if the doors of rooms are left open. Those rooms you don't use—and there must be quite a few in a house of this size with only two of you living in it—can be kept closed and that will help to direct the warm currents to where you need them. Bedrooms, bathroom, staircase, hall—everywhere. Besides, I'm sure you'll agree, if the hall is warm the whole house is.'

He showed Nancy and herself photographs of the unit, and it looked a most pleasing piece of equipment.

'It's the most economical form of heating I know,' Geoffrey Hunt told her. 'It can be regulated, left on safely all night or when you go out for an evening, and it's absolutely trouble-free.'

Both Vanessa and Nancy were won over. As the kitchen was farthest away from the hall and also had a fireplace, he suggested that a small unit in there in addition to the larger one in the hall would make for even greater comfort.

'Don't make up your mind right away. Chew it over, and give me a ring,' he told Vanessa. 'But don't leave it too long, otherwise we shall get too busy and there might be a long delay.'

He said hire purchase could be arranged, and it all sounded too good to be true. He advised the same kind of unit for the barn, even though this had no chimney. The pipe in that case could be taken through a hole in the wall and up outside. If Vanessa did not like the appearance, an outside chimney could be built on some time. He suggested electric heating for the greenhouse, and promised to send an estimate for the whole operation.

The estimate arrived within a few days, and both Nancy and Vanessa were amazed at the low price. Nancy had insisted that she should pay half the cost, which meant the project would be well within Vanessa's resources.

'It's so cheap, I'm beginning to doubt whether it can be really efficient,' she said to Nancy.

'I'm sure it will be, myself. In any case most forms of central heating only give a sort of background warmth. And that's really all that's necessary. The kitchen will be well taken care of and we can still have open fires or additional electric fires in the rooms we use in the evenings—and your study in very cold weather. But if you're in doubt, why not ask Ian Hamilton's advice?'

'Yes, perhaps I will—though he's awfully elusive these days. Every time I ring either Cecile Harland answers the phone or Ian isn't in.'

'How many times, in actual fact?' Nancy quizzed. 'And it could be just a coincidence that Miss Harland happens to have been paying them a visit.'

'It isn't a coincidence that he takes her out to dinner,' Vanessa answered without thinking.

Nancy eyed her keenly. 'And how many times has he taken her out to dinner, to your certain knowledge?'

Vanessa had to admit that it was only once. 'But I daresay there have been plenty of other occasions.'

'You're only guessing,' Nancy told her. 'And it's my belief that you're exaggerating, too.'

'Maybe.'

Several times that day Vanessa reached for the telephone to ring Ian, then changed her mind. Perhaps she had exaggerated about the number of occasions Ian had taken Cecile out and was jumping to conclusions altogether about his relationship with her, but there was no doubt about his silence. It was weeks since she had either heard from him or seen him. Not since, in fact, the day he had called and found Miles standing with his arm about her shoulders. Freda's explanation of the engagement ring had made not the slightest difference.

But on a sudden decision the following morning when she went into her study after breakfast, she dialled his number. Cecile surely couldn't be there at this hour unless she had stayed the night or was indeed living there.

Her heart seemed to leap into her throat as Ian himself answered the phone.

'Oh, Ian, this is Vanessa.'

There was a second of silence. Then his voice came cool and impersonal.

'Yes, Vanessa? What can I do for you?'

Her courage almost failed her. Apart from his mention of her name, she might have been a complete stranger to him.

'I—wanted to thank you for sending the heating engineer,' she said, sure that her trembling voice would give her away.

'That's all right,' he answered in the same detached voice. 'Did you find his estimate satisfactory?'

'That's what I rang you about. It's so cheap I can't be sure it will be any good.'

'That's one of the surest attitudes I know of helping to keep prices high,' he said in an exasperated tone. 'What kind of heating did he suggest?'

Slightly taken aback by his remark, she gave him more details.

'It all sounds very satisfactory to my mind,' he said when she had finished. 'You can take it from me, Geoff Hunt is an upright and honest business man. That's why I sent him to you. And it so happens that Puck's Hill is just the right sort of house for that form of heating. I think you'll find it cheap to run and very efficient. The reason it's so cheap is that installation is so simple. It doesn't entail the whole house being torn apart.'

'So you'd advise me to go ahead with it?'

'I certainly would. The only tricky part might be in the lighting of that kind of unit. You mustn't let too much oil get into the bowl at first. Turn it up gradually, otherwise pressure builds up in the flue and you get a terrific noise. It's not dangerous, just alarming. But Geoff Hunt will show you.'

' Thanks. Thanks very much, Ian.'

' That's all right. Any time,' he answered casually.

There was a pause. Vanessa hoped he would say something else, something of a more personal or friendly nature, even if only to ask how the garden business was doing, but he didn't, and there was little else she could do except say goodbye and ring off. Ringing him had given her no personal satisfaction whatever. She had run away from one hopeless love affair only to become involved in another. But this time she was not going to recover quite so easily—if ever.

Day after day Vanessa opened up her shop for customers, worked in the garden and tended her plants. The heating was installed, and noticeably the hours of daylight grew shorter with the approach of autumn. Now and then when the people of the village came to buy some item for their gardens, they stayed to chat and marvel at the progress Vanessa had made in so short a time. Miraculously, it seemed, the giant hogweed, the *Heracleum mantegazzianum*, had gone, and in its place, stretches of green turf which Joe kept rough-cut with the aid of a rotary mower. Occasionally, Freda breezed in, or Vanessa met her in town for lunch, but Ian continued to hold himself aloof. Occasionally, too, Miles called to see her. Once or twice he asked her out, but she always declined, and whenever he tried to put his arm around her, as he sometimes did, she was invariably firm with him.

One evening when there was a sharp drop in temperature, she and Nancy decided to test out their heating. Very carefully, Vanessa followed the instructions the heating engineer had given her, and very soon the whole house was pleasantly warm. Miles called that evening and displayed a very great interest in the unit.

' Marvellous idea,' he said. ' Who put you on to it?'

' Ian sent a man called Hunt,' she told him.

' Ah, clever Ian,' he said sarcastically. ' Do you see much of him nowadays?'

' I've been busy—and so has he, I imagine,' she answered.

Miles very obviously suppressed a smile. ' Well, I'm pleased to know he doesn't get all his way.'

Vanessa turned on him. ' Miles, if you're going to be unpleasant, I'd rather you left.'

' But, darling girl, I only—'

' And don't call me '' darling girl ''!'

He shrugged. ' All right, all right.' He turned to go, then turned, his face serious. ' Vanessa, you're not very happy, are you? And I guess it's something to do with Hamilton. I hate to say this, but he's hooked on Cecile and I think you know that. Why don't you get out of here, sell the place and have yourself enough money to travel or something? Either that or marry me. You could do a lot worse, you know. You might not think you love me enough at the moment, but I'm told by some of my married pals that love often comes after marriage.'

Vanessa took a deep breath. What a simple solution it sounded! But she shook her head slowly.

' No, Miles, I can't, but thanks all the same. I know how you feel about me keeping my promise to Aunt Maud, but I feel I must. And I can't marry you feeling as I do about—someone else.'

' People are falling in and out of love all the time. It doesn't last for ever, especially when it's one-sided. One of these days you'll fall out of love with him, and it might happen sooner than you think. But if you don't want to marry me, how about selling Puck's Hill to me? You'd be better away from here.'

' Please don't say any more, Miles. Even if I did

167

ever leave Puck's Hill I'd never sell it.'

He left then, but what he had said had unsettled her. For weeks she had tried not to think about Ian, to keep herself busy, to be so tired night after night that she was falling to sleep as she mounted the stairs to bed. But now she was suddenly defenceless. Was it true? Was Ian really 'hooked on' Cecile? Vanessa almost groaned aloud. What was she to do? She couldn't go on like this indefinitely. She could not sell Puck's Hill, she thought suddenly, but she had not made any promises about not giving it away. She could give it to Nancy. Surely Aunt Maud would not have minded that? Vanessa didn't think that would be compromising. In fact, she need not actually give it to Nancy. She could simply let her live here, have whomsoever she wished to live with her. Nancy might even be able to find a man to manage the garden business and so keep that on. It was beginning to pay now, and would be even more profitable when her pot plants were coming into flower and ready for sale—which would be fairly soon now. Many of them were already potted up. Some people liked to buy them for some weeks before Christmas and bring them into actual flower themselves.

Yet somehow she knew she did not want to go away. Wherever she went she would never stop loving Ian. She began to think about him properly, recalling the Sunday she had lunched at the Lodge, the evening at the Foresters' Club before the incident of the ring. Surely he didn't dislike her as much as she imagined? Hadn't he said she was worth wooing and pursuing? It was true that she had been antagonistic towards him at first and this had caused her to often be rude to him and resent him, so she herself was at fault, if indeed he did dislike her. But Freda had said emphatically that he *didn't*, and he had certainly gone out of his way to help her.

She decided she would not give up without a fight.

Freda herself had said there were a whole heap of things which needed clearing up between Ian and Vanessa. The first thing to do was really find out whether there *was* anything between Ian and Cecile. If there wasn't, she would do all she could to *make* Ian like her. In any event she simply had to find out the truth.

In the morning she rang the Lodge, and this time it was Freda who answered.

'Freda, may I come along to see you and Ian this evening?'

'Yes, of course,' Freda answered swiftly. 'Although Ian has to go out. Would you like to come and have a meal with us or—'

But perhaps it would be better to talk to Freda first, so Vanessa said she would not go for a meal but be there about eight o'clock.

'Nice to see you,' Freda greeted her. 'Sorry if we appear to have been neglecting you. Is there something special or did you just want to get out for an hour or so?'

'No, it's a little more than that. I felt I had to come. You see, I'm thinking of going away—probably back home.'

The announcement startled Freda. 'But why? Just as you're doing so well with your garden centre and everything?'

Freda led her into the sitting room where she had some coffee waiting.

'I think, Freda, you must know why,' Vanessa said quietly. 'But there are one or two things I simply must find out before I make up my mind finally.'

'Anything I *can* tell you, Vanessa, I will,' Freda told her. 'But you must understand I can't tell you anything I know Ian wouldn't want me to.'

'Just answer me two questions, Freda, if you can. First, does Cecile Harland really mean anything to Ian? Is he going to marry her? Or would he like to?'

'I wouldn't think so. Ian has been advising her

father about his trees—they have quite an estate. We knew the family before we came here to live.'

'Miles says he followed her here and that he's—in love with her.'

Freda's eyes widened. 'How could Miles Kendal possibly know, in any case? He's a thoroughly bad lot, that man, and I'm glad you've given him the go-by. Anyhow, it simply isn't true that Ian followed her here. It was a sheer coincidence. He's only taken her out once—and that was the time you saw them. She's been here once or twice, and it's probable that she'd like to see more of Ian, but—'

Vanessa felt she was likely to burst with a sudden feeling of joy and excitement, but she took herself firmly in hand.

'The other thing, Freda, is—what does Ian *really* think of me?'

Freda passed her a cup of coffee and the sugar. 'Now that *is* a difficult question, Vanessa, and I don't think I can answer it.'

'Does he hate me?'

'Good heavens, no. What a question!'

'Dislike me, then?'

'No, of course not.'

'Then—then why is he avoiding me? Why doesn't he drop in at Puck's Hill like he used to?'

'Vanessa, I can't tell you. How can I? I doubt even if Ian himself would—' She broke off, clearly ill at ease. 'Look, Vanessa, I know how you feel and what a difficult time you must be going through. And believe me, I only wish I could do something about it. But this is something you and Ian will have to work out for yourselves.'

'Work out for *ourselves*?' repeated Vanessa in a puzzled voice. 'Why do you say that?'

Freda sighed and put her hand to her head. 'Vanessa, don't ask me any more questions, please. I told Ian how the engagement ring happened to be in your bag, and that you weren't engaged to Miles, and he believes that. Now, I've set *your* mind at rest about Cecile. More than that I can't do. But you must understand, it's very difficult for Ian.'

Vanessa could scarcely grasp the significance of what Freda was saying and what she was implying. She felt too utterly bewildered.

'What's—difficult for Ian?' she asked breathlessly, her voice barely above a whisper. Then, as she received an admonishing look from Freda: 'I'm sorry, you said no more questions. But, Freda, I must know—please!'

But Freda shook her head. 'My dear, you'll just have to be patient. I only fear one thing—that whatever Ian's feelings are, he might never ask you to marry him.'

Vanessa would not have been able to describe her feelings at that moment. Fear, elation and despair screwed themselves into a tight, painful knot inside her.

'But—but why? Why not? What makes you say such a thing?'

But a very determined look settled on Freda's face. 'Sorry, I mustn't say any more. I've said more than enough already.'

'You—don't think I've been silly or lacking in pride to come and talk to you like this?'

'Good heavens, no. I only hope things will work out—for both of you. I certainly wouldn't be in too much of a hurry to leave, if I were you. How long is it now since you came, by the way? Or rather, since your aunt died?'

Vanessa sighed. She felt drained and could not even think straight. How long it was since she had left home or since she had been the owner of Puck's Hill seemed entirely irrelevant and unimportant.

'It must be nearly six months, I suppose.'

'I think it is. In which case you might soon come into the other money your aunt left for you. Have you ever wondered what the conditions might be?'

Vanessa shook her head. 'I've no idea. Aunt Maud was a little unpredictable at times.'

'Maybe she wanted to see how you'd make out—what you'd do with Puck's Hill. The solicitor did say it was a great deal of money, didn't he? And if the condition *was* anything to do with Puck's Hill—well, there'd be no doubt that you'd qualify. You've done absolute wonders there.'

'Ian suggested that it might be a condition that I shouldn't marry.'

'Did he? And what did you say to that?'

'What would any girl in her right mind say? Love means a good deal more than money.'

Freda's look softened. 'Well, I think you've got plenty to chew over during the next week or so, anyway. Once you can see Ian's point of view, it might be up to you to take the initiative. And don't ask me to explain that,' she added quickly. 'Just think about it all.'

'Think about it all? My mind boggles. I only hope I come up with the right answers.'

They had talked longer than either of them realized, so that when they heard Ian's key in the lock they were both startled.

'Heavens, I shouldn't be here,' Vanessa said, jumping to her feet. 'I meant to be gone before he came back.'

'Calm down. It's probably for the best,' Freda told her. 'But he's certainly home sooner than I expected.'

Vanessa met him in the hall. Her heart contracted painfully, and she thought how tired and strained he looked.

'Hello, Vanessa,' he said. 'I thought that was your car outside.'

'I'm just going, actually,' she told him.

'You don't have to on my account,' he said stiffly. 'I

shall probably go straight on upstairs anyway.'

With difficulty Vanessa let hurt feelings bounce straight off her.

She reiterated her intention of going. 'Won't you—see me to my car, Ian?' she found herself saying. 'There are one or two things I want to say to you.'

He eyed her suspiciously. 'What sort of things?'

'Please, Ian.'

Freda looked from one to the other uncertainly. Then she said swiftly:

'I'll go and put some coffee on, Ian, and make some sandwiches.'

She disappeared quickly into the kitchen. Silently, Vanessa blessed her. She was determined now to use and to take advantage of every possible opportunity to fight for her love. She called out goodnight to Freda, then moved towards the door. Ian had little option but to follow her. But outside, he opened her car door and held it open as if very anxious to be rid of her. But for the talk she had had with Freda, Vanessa's pride would have prevailed and her courage wavered. Now, she smiled up at him.

'It's nice to see you again, Ian. I've—missed you dropping in to see me and—sort of bullying me.'

He frowned and did not speak for a minute, then he said: 'Are you trying to flirt with me, Vanessa?'

She met his gaze, and the urge to put her arms about his neck was strong.

'No, Ian, I'm not,' she answered. 'I'm serious. I've come to my senses at last.'

Taking a chance, she reached one hand up to his shoulder and raised her face to his.

His expression alerted. He gripped her arms fiercely. 'Vanessa, what are you talking about? What are you trying to say?'

But suddenly the whole sky was lit with a red glow. Startled, they looked in the direction from which it came, and Vanessa's eyes dilated as a great tongue of flame seemed to rise from the trees.

'Ian— It's Puck's Hill! It's on fire—and Nancy's in there alone!'

CHAPTER IX

Without thinking, Vanessa started to run in the direction of the boundary fence, her one thought to get to Nancy quickly.

'Vanessa—Vanessa, not that way!'

Ian caught her up. He grasped hold of her and made her stop.

'Vanessa, it's quicker by car, it really is. I'll get to her. You go inside and telephone the fire brigade. They can't have been sent for yet, or we'd have heard the siren.'

He gave her a push in the direction of the house, then ran towards his car. Distressed as she was, she realized the truth of what he had said. It *was* quicker by car. As she rushed into the house, she heard Ian's car start up with a roar.

'Freda—'

'What on earth—'

'Freda, quick, let me use the phone. Puck's Hill is on fire!'

She dialled 999 and gave the address in a voice that shook, then clamped the receiver down again.

'Was that Ian's car I heard going down the drive?' queried Freda.

Vanessa nodded and ran to the door. Freda followed her, and together they drove as quickly as possible to the house. As the car turned into the drive the fire siren wailed out on the night air like a monster suddenly released, and the next moment the clang of the engine could be heard.

As soon as Vanessa was out of the car she rushed to the front door but was driven back as thick smoke billowed out.

Freda ran after her and took hold of her arm.

'Vanessa, don't go in. Ian must be there. He'll get Nancy out.'

'But—but how?— Unless he got in at the back?'

She ran round to the back door, but that was locked, and through the window she could see fire licking up the legs of the tables and chairs. Vanessa picked up a brick to break open a window and get in that way, but Freda stopped her.

'If you introduce more air, you'll make it worse. The only thing to do is wait for the fire brigade. They'll know the right thing to do.'

As Freda spoke the urgent clanging became louder and louder, and in a matter of minutes the fire engine rushed up the drive. But Vanessa's fears were for Ian and Nancy. What was keeping them? Had they been overcome by the heat and smoke? Instinctively, she moved towards the house again, but Freda caught hold of her.

'Vanessa, you mustn't. I know how you feel—Ian *is* my brother, but he'll be all right, I—I'm sure.'

But Vanessa felt her panic rising, and to go in after him and Nancy was an urge too strong to be fought down. She shook herself free of Freda's restraining hand and rushed to the door. Again she was choked back by the volume of smoke and the fierce heat, but she braced herself and, head down, rushed blindly into the hall. Flames licked the stairs and banister. It would be impossible to get either up or down. Vanessa made an effort to call Ian's name, but as she opened her mouth and inhaled, she was choked by the thick, billowing smoke. She coughed violently and tears streamed from her eyes. Her senses swam and a feeling of failure hit her forcibly. She made for the stairs again and tried to call out, *Ian—Ian—*

Now her tears were real and not simply caused by the smoke. She had failed. Ian was somewhere in the burning house, someone was holding her back, trying to stop her from reaching him.

'Ian—Ian—'

Then by some miracle she was in Ian's arms and he was talking to her in a low, urgent, almost incoherent voice. She thought he called her 'darling', but couldn't be sure. There was so much noise all around and other voices intruding. Cold night air struck her face and she opened her eyes to find Ian's face within inches of her own.

'Vanessa! Vanessa, are you all right?' he queried anxiously.

She was so relieved to see him, she broke into a sob, repeating his name as she had in what she knew now was a dream of unconsciousness, and still in a half-dream, half-awake state her arms went around his neck.

'Ian! Oh, darling, I'm so glad you're safe!'

She sensed rather than felt him stiffen, and not until she felt her feet touch the ground did she realize that she had been held in his arms. Her brain rapidly clearing, she rubbed her eyes and looked about her.

'Nancy! Where's Nancy? Is she all right?'

Ian took her arm. 'Yes, she's all right. Freda is with her in the shooting-brake. We got out through a bedroom window in the time-honoured fashion of knotting sheets together. I can understand your anxiety, but it was foolish of you to go inside. The best thing you can do now is to go back to our place, both you and Nancy, and stay the night. Freda will go with you. I'll stay here until the fire's out. The firemen will soon have it under control, I think. There's damage, of course, particularly to the stairs and in the kitchen, but the place won't be entirely burned out.'

He led her to the shooting-brake gently, but in a way which clearly expected no argument. Vanessa looked back at the house, reluctant to leave, but Ian opened the door on the passenger side and pushed her firmly on to the seat, picking up her legs and planting them inside after her. Then he slammed the door. Nancy was on the rear seat. Freda was already at the wheel, and before Vanessa could begin to argue she had started the engine and was driving away.

Vanessa sighed, realizing the futility of protesting, and admitting to herself that Ian was right as usual.

'Don't worry, Vanessa,' Freda said, guessing some of her thoughts. 'Ian will see to everything. You can rely on him.'

'Yes, I know.' Vanessa turned to Nancy and asked if she were all right. Mercifully, she was.

'It was just that I couldn't get down the stairs,' she said. 'I simply had to pray that sooner or later somebody would see the fire and call the fire brigade. I knew you weren't far away.'

'You'd gone to bed then, when it started?'

'Yes, I read a bit and then fell asleep. I heard a noise and went on to the landing—but already flames were leaping upstairs and the whole place was filled with smoke. I can't *think* how it started. Everything was all right when I went upstairs.'

'What about the heaters? Were they on high? Although, even if they were, I can't see—'

But Nancy said she had turned them both low. It was a mystery and was likely to remain so unless the firemen had any explanations or theory to propose.

When they arrived at the Lodge, Freda insisted on both Vanessa and Nancy going straight upstairs to bed while she made hot drinks to take up to them.

'You must both be in a state of shock, even though you might not realize it,' she said. 'When Ian comes back I'll let you know how things are, if you're still awake.'

Vanessa did not argue. After Nancy, she had a bath to remove the smell of smoke, and even as she slipped into bed Freda reported from her own bedroom window that the flames from Puck's Hill had died down completely.

But Vanessa had more to keep her awake than the fire. Thoughts of Ian occupied her mind, her conversation with Freda, and everything she had said about Ian. Most of all, his murmured 'darling' when he thought she was unconscious. Had she been dreaming or not? Freda had said that Ian would never ask her to marry him. Was it possible, was it remotely probable that Ian loved her, but the question of her inheritance was holding him back? She told herself that this was presuming a terrible lot. Suppose she were wrong? She tried to think back, to search her mind for any signs that Ian might feel the same about her as she did about him. They were only too rare. With few exceptions all she had to go on were Freda's hints. But she decided that whatever the outcome she must make some effort to find out the truth of his regard, or lack of it for her, by subtle or direct means. Her own pride was a matter of no importance now. And Ian's? Perhaps she should at least give him the opportunity of telling her how he felt first.

She was thinking about what she should say to him when she heard his car and a few minutes later, voices downstairs, his own and Freda's. Vanessa got out of bed quickly and put on a dressing gown she found behind the door. Ian and Freda were talking in the hall and looked up as she appeared.

'It's all right, Vanessa,' Ian told her. 'It's out now. The firemen made sure of that. And I've locked the doors and windows.'

She walked slowly down the stairs. 'Thanks for what you did, Ian. Is there much damage?'

'It could have been worse. But I should go back to bed, if I were you. We can talk about it in the morning, and I'll go over there with you first thing.'

She had reached the bottom stair and stood with her hand on the curved banister rail.

'I'm sorry if I made extra trouble for you by rushing inside,' she told him. 'I was so worried—not only about Nancy, but about you.'

As she spoke she felt her cheeks colouring and her heartbeat quicken, but she stood her ground and waited for his reaction.

He gave her an unsmiling glance. 'You—gave us all some anxious moments,' he said, 'but it's over now, and I hope nothing like that ever happens again. Good-night, Vanessa.'

Freda asked her if she'd like another drink, and Ian took the opportunity of disappearing into the kitchen. But with a heavy heart Vanessa went back to bed. It was not going to be easy to talk to Ian.

The house had been quiet for a very long time before she finally drifted off to sleep. As a consequence she slept late, and when she went down to breakfast he had already eaten and was outside working. Nancy was having her breakfast in bed.

'She doesn't seem any the worse,' Freda said. 'What about you?'

Vanessa said she was fine and asked about Ian. Freda smiled.

'He put his coat over his head when he dashed up the stairs to Nancy—and later when he went in after you. So he hasn't suffered any damage. Between ourselves,' she added, 'he was pretty frantic when he knew you were inside.'

'Really?' asked Vanessa eagerly. 'It's so difficult to know what Ian is thinking.'

'That's because he's doing his best to hide his feelings. You'll have to be very persistent, Vanessa,' Freda told her quietly.

After breakfast Ian left his work and drove Vanessa to Puck's Hill. She thought he must be very adept indeed at hiding his feelings. It was difficult to believe that he had been remotely 'frantic' for her safety the previous night. After a brief enquiry as to how she was feeling after her ordeal he was grim-faced and distant.

Vanessa was appalled at the damage to the staircase. The treads of the stairway were charred, the walls blackened, the banister burnt almost through.

'I'm afraid it won't be safe for you to go upstairs, Vanessa,' Ian said. 'You'll have to stay with us for the time being. Nancy too, of course.'

To Vanessa, the way he put it made her feel she was being a nuisance, and some of her old pride asserted itself.

'There's no "have to" about it, Ian,' she answered. 'I can stay somewhere in the village—the Stag, perhaps. Or maybe go home.'

'Home?' he echoed sharply. 'But what about your business—and Nancy?'

'I can sell the stock and put an end to the business, or maybe get a manager in. And Nancy can have some-one to live with her. Don't worry about the house. I shall never *sell* Puck's Hill,' she added swiftly.

He frowned. 'You talk as if you intend leaving Barn Hill for good. Hadn't you better wait until you hear from Mr Oliver, the solicitor?'

There was not the slightest bit of regret in his voice that she might be leaving. She almost groaned aloud. She had not intended saying the kind of things to him that she had. An eternity seemed to pass in which Ian was being drawn further and further away from her until he was no more than a distant speck.

'Ian—' she said with swift, sharp urgency.

'Yes?' He looked at her oddly. 'Is something wrong?'

She brought herself swiftly from her fantasy. But it was a fantasy which had served as a warning, that if she did not take care, she would certainly lose Ian because of her own stupid pride.

'No, no, there's nothing wrong. I—shall be glad to stay with you and Freda for a little while, thank you, if you're sure I won't be an inconvenience. But I'd like to talk to you some time, Ian.'

'What about?'

'Not now. Let's go and look at the kitchen.'

Here the whole place was black—walls, ceiling, floor, the cooker and sink unit. The table was burnt and charred, the curtains completely destroyed. Vanessa sniffed.

'Ian, I can smell paraffin.'

He nodded. 'So could the firemen last night. And the two heating units were turned up as high as they could be.'

'Nancy says she turned them low and that everything was all right when she went to bed.'

'In any case—and I've been on the phone to Geoff—no matter how high the units had been they wouldn't have caused fire to break out. And there's no smell of paraffin ever with them.'

It was true. 'Then how on earth could it have happened?' puzzled Vanessa.

'That's probably what the police will find out.'

'The police?'

'Oh yes. They automatically investigate the cause of fires. If a cause can't be found, then arson is suspected —and that's a very serious matter.'

'Arson?' Vanessa echoed again. 'But who on earth—'

Even as she spoke there came a knock at the front door, and Vanessa opened it to a police sergeant. He asked questions and took a good look around then asked more questions.

'Who knew you'd had these heating units put in besides yourselves—and, of course, the heating engineer?' he asked.

'I don't know. Very few people, I think,' she

answered. 'Mr Hamilton and his sister, of course, and —yes, Miles Kendal.'

'Miles Kendal, the property developer?' the sergeant asked sharply.

'Why, yes, but—'

'Any of these people might have to be questioned,' he said. 'But first of all, I must speak to Miss Gould. I understand she was in the house alone at the time.'

The whole thing was now emerging as something quite alarming. Vanessa did not like it one bit. If only Nancy had left some clothes airing or something simple like that! But Vanessa knew that she hadn't, nor would she ever. She was far too sensible and conscientious.

Vanessa opened her 'shop' and Ian and the police sergeant went to the Lodge, the sergeant to interview Nancy. Later, Nancy joined her at Puck's Hill and did her best to clean up the cooker and sink. The kitchen would need completely redecorating and the furniture replacing with new. Nancy wanted to pay for these herself, but Vanessa would not hear of it, though at present she could not see how she was going to be able to afford either a new kitchen or staircase which would include, also, hall and landing.

The whole affair was depressing beyond measure, particularly as the police decided that the fire was not an accident, but a result of arson. Someone was suspected of forcing open the lock of the front door by means of a picklock, and throwing paraffin over the stair carpet, banister, hall carpet and curtains—the same in the kitchen. Whoever it was had then turned up the heating units to make it appear like an accident—not knowing this would be impossible—then left open the front door and set a match to the paraffin. The police also interviewed Joe, the two men who had helped with the weed clearance, and Miles. The greatest suspect was Miles, but he denied being near the house on the night of the fire, as did the other men interviewed.

'I'd rather it were *not* proved,' Vanessa said to Ian that evening. 'It's too horrible to think about.'

She knew that Ian and Freda as well as Nancy thought Miles both capable and guilty. He so badly wanted to buy Puck's Hill and thought to force Vanessa's hand. Vanessa thought it likely too, but she did not want to think about it. Perhaps he hadn't meant to harm Nancy, only to scare herself. He must have seen her go out and waited his opportunity, and watched for Nancy's light going on upstairs. But the important thing to Vanessa was finding out how she stood in Ian's eyes. That evening when Nancy had retired and Freda was upstairs in her room Vanessa tried to discuss things with him.

'Ian, can we have our little talk now?' she began.

'Of course. What is it?'

She quailed at the cool politeness in his voice, but went on: 'First, I want to apologize for all the times when I've seemed—difficult. I'm—not usually so.'

His expression was guarded. 'There isn't the slightest need for you to apologize about anything, Vanessa. We all have periods when we're not quite at our best, myself included.'

'But you were being so kind and helpful. You must have thought me terribly ungrateful.'

'Not in the least,' he answered.

Vanessa almost despaired. This was getting her absolutely nowhere. She tried another tack.

'Ian, would you be sorry if I left Barn Hill for good?'

She watched him start, then freeze. 'You must do just what you think best, Vanessa. I can only repeat what I said to you this morning. Wait until you've heard from Mr Oliver.'

'Yes, I'll do that,' she answered quietly. 'But whether I go or stay depends entirely upon you.'

He frowned and glanced at her swiftly. 'What do you mean? Why does it depend on me?'

'I want to know what you think of me, Ian.'

At this he rose swiftly to his feet and stood on the hearth, his back turned towards her.

'Why should you want to know that? And what possible difference can it make?'

'All the difference in the world,' she answered softly. She stood up and went towards him and put her hand on his shoulder. 'You see, I—think a very great deal of you.'

He swung round and stared at her with wide eyes, his skin stretched taut across his jawbone.

'Vanessa, don't say things like that!'

'But I must. And I must know how it is with you. I—feel about you, Ian, as I've never felt about any man before.'

He backed away from her. 'Please, Vanessa, don't say any more, I beg of you. It's impossible. I can't. You don't know what you're saying or what you're asking. The best thing you can do is to go back home and forget all about me.'

He went out, and Vanessa sank into a chair feeling sick at heart. If he'd loved her he would have told her so. It would have been better if she had said nothing. She went out into the hall and heard his footsteps on the front verandah, then the crunch of his feet on the gravel outside. Evidently he was going for a walk through his grounds.

Vanessa went out too. She couldn't possibly stay at the Lodge now. She got in her car and drove back to Puck's Hill. She would sleep on the settee if the stairs really proved unsafe. When she arrived she telephoned from her study—a room the fire had not reached, and told Freda where she was. Freda protested and argued, but Vanessa was firm. Ian knew how she felt about him now. If he loved her he would seek her out.

She slept little that night, and it was not due in the least to any discomfort of the settee. She had not bothered to test the stairs, after all. She had felt too utterly miserable.

In the morning a letter was delivered from the solicitor asking her to call and see him in his office in a few days time. She would stay at Puck's Hill until then, she decided, then leave Nancy to do what she liked with the house. She would not sell it nor give it away. She would 'lend' it to Nancy.

Both Freda and Nancy came to see her to try to persuade her to go back to the Lodge, but when Nancy saw Vanessa was adamant, she insisted on returning too. They discovered that by treading the stairs carefully along the side by the wall, it was possible to go up. Nancy refused to discuss the future at all until Vanessa had seen the solicitor, and in vain Vanessa told her that it would make no difference. She still intended to go away.

She did not see Ian at all, but Freda called each day, and though Vanessa felt as though her heart would break, she was beyond tears. All she felt was a coldness, and in her heart a dull ache.

Without much interest she drove into town to the solicitor's office.

'Ah, Miss Woodrow.' Mr Oliver shook hands with her and invited her to sit down. 'The six-month period your aunt wanted to pass before you received your inheritance is up today. I've had a good talk with my fellow trustee, and we have decided that you have indeed fulfilled all the conditions.'

'But what *were* the conditions? And how can you possibly know whether I've fulfilled them or not? You haven't seen me since the day I came into your office six months ago.'

'Ah, but I know all about what you've been doing,' he told her mysteriously. 'But before we go any further, I think you should meet my fellow trustee. He's in another office. He'll tell you all about it. This way, if you don't mind.'

He led her into the corridor and opened a door for her. 'There you are, Miss Woodrow.'

He allowed her to precede him, or so she thought, but instead he closed the door after her, and she was left alone with a man who stood with his back to her, looking out of the window. Vanessa's heart leapt violently.

'Ian!'

He turned. 'Yes, I'm the other trustee, Vanessa,' he said in answer to the unspoken question in her eyes. 'And now perhaps you will understand how impossible it is for me to—take you up on what you were saying the other evening.'

She stared at him, trying to fit the pieces of the jigsaw together in her mind, but it was difficult all at once.

'No, I don't think I do understand quite,' she answered.

He sighed. 'It's simple enough. Your aunt has left you a great deal of money and, of course, as a trustee I was well aware how much it was. I also knew the conditions. They were that you would do something worthwhile with Puck's Hill, that you would not use chemical weed-killer to clear the giant hogweed, and altogether prove yourself worthy of your inheritance. Now do you see?'

'I see your difficulty. How much money is it exactly?'

'Twenty thousand pounds all told.'

Vanessa gasped. 'Good heavens! I *am* beginning to see.'

'I thought you might. But of course, it wasn't much of a gamble on your aunt's part. She knew you well enough. And so there you are. You're a very rich woman, Vanessa, and I couldn't possibly take advantage of the fact.'

'I'm not asking you to.' Vanessa moved towards him. Now she knew what Freda had meant when she said Ian would never ask her to marry him. 'All I'm asking is that you answer me truthfully. Do you care for me, Ian? At all?'

He took a deep breath. 'Of course I care for you,' he shot out. 'I would have thought it only too obvious.'

'You mean you love me?' she persisted.

He closed his eyes momentarily, then opened them and looked past her.

'Yes, but I'm not going to ask you to marry me.'

'Then I'm asking *you*.'

'No, Vanessa! Don't you see?'

'No, I don't. But what I do see is a very selfish man. Don't you care that if I can't marry you I shall be the unhappiest woman alive? That I shall remain unhappy for the rest of my life? Is that what you want? Is it, Ian?'

He groaned. 'Vanessa, don't. You'll forget me in time, just as I—' He broke off, lines of pain etched deeply across his face.

'Just as you will forget me? Is that what you were going to say? Will you forget me, Ian, " in time "?'

The next moment she was crushed in his arms, his lips hard on hers.

'Vanessa, forgive me. I love you so much it hurts. I would never forget you, ever. Not for as long as I lived.'

Tears misted her eyes. 'I'll give the money away if you like, all of it,' she murmured, her whole being on fire with the love she had for him.

'Do what you like with it. Do what you like, darling Vanessa, only marry me—please, for I know I simply couldn't live without you.'

Locked in his arms, his lips on hers, Vanessa caught a sudden vision of Aunt Maud's face, puckish and mischievous.

'To my dear niece, Ian Hamilton—to have and to hold—'

And suddenly she knew that this was what her aunt had intended from the very beginning.

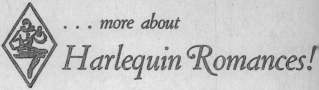

. . . more about

Harlequin Romances!

If you enjoyed reading this Harlequin Romance, or if you are a devoted Harlequin reader from way back — and would like a listing of other Harlequin Romances, possibly not available from your local bookseller, you can receive our FREE catalogue by completing and mailing the coupon below.

Here is a wonderful opportunity to read the many Harlequin Romances you've missed, and add to your private library.

Simply fill out the coupon below, mail it to us and we'll rush your FREE catalogue to you!

Following this page you'll find a sampling of a few of the HARLEQUIN ROMANCES listed in the catalogue. Should you wish to order any of these immediately, kindly check the titles desired and mail with coupon.

HARLEQUIN READER SERVICE
84 Ballantyne Avenue
Stratford, Ontario, Canada

☐ Please send me the free Harlequin Romance Catalogue.

☐ Please send me the titles checked on the back.

I enclose $_____ (Cheque or Money Order—no currency or C.O.D.'s please). All books are 50c each; if less than 6 books, add 10c per book for postage and handling.

Name _____

Address _____

City _____

State or Prov. _____ Zip_____

Have You Missed Any of These
Harlequin Romances?

- ☐ 626 NURSE TRENT'S CHILDREN
  Joyce Dingwell
- ☐ 1070 THE DRUMMER OF CORRAE
  Jean S. Macleod
- ☐ 1076 BELLS IN THE WIND
  Kate Starr
- ☐ 1089 HOSPITAL BY THE LAKE
  Anne Durham
- ☐ 1100 THE BROKEN WING
  Mary Burchell
- ☐ 1108 SUMMER EVERY DAY
  Jane Arbor
- ☐ 1116 PLAY THE TUNE SOFTLY
  Amanda Doyle
- ☐ 1125 DARLING RHADAMANTHUS
  Margery Hilton
- ☐ 1145 YOUNG DOCTOR YERDLEY
  Anne Durham
- ☐ 1168 ROSE IN THE BUD
  Susan Barrie
- ☐ 1170 RED LOTUS
  Catherine Airlie
- ☐ 1172 LET LOVE ABIDE
  Norrey Ford
- ☐ 1175 MOON OVER MADRID
  Fiona Finlay
- ☐ 1181 DANGEROUS LOVE
  Jane Beaufort
- ☐ 1185 WHEN DOCTORS MEET
  Juliet Shore
- ☐ 1192 THE CERTAIN SPRING
  Nan Asquith
- ☐ 1194 SUNSHINE YELLOW
  Mary Whistler
- ☐ 1198 HAPPY EVER AFTER
  Dorothy Rivers
- ☐ 1211 BRIDE OF KYLSAIG
  Iris Danbury
- ☐ 1228 THE YOUNG NIGHTINGALES
  Mary Whistler
- ☐ 1232 A DAY LIKE SPRING
  Jane Fraser
- ☐ 1235 LOVE AS IT FLIES
  Marguerite Lees
- ☐ 1241 NURSE BARLOW'S JINX
  Marjorie Norrell
- ☐ 1246 THE CONSTANT HEART
  Eleanor Farnes
- ☐ 1250 THE SAFFRON SKY
  Isobel Chace

- ☐ 1255 LITTLE SAVAGE
  Margaret Malcolm
- ☐ 1258 NOBODY'S CHILD
  Catherine Airlie
- ☐ 1259 WILD SONATA
  Susan Barrie
- ☐ 1264 SECRET STAR
  Marguerite Lees
- ☐ 1274 MAN FROM THE SEA
  Pamela Kent
- ☐ 1282 THE SHINING STAR
  Hilary Wilde
- ☐ 1283 ROSALIND COMES HOME
  Essie Summers
- ☐ 1301 HOTEL BY THE LOCH
  Iris Danbury
- ☐ 1304 SHARLIE FOR SHORT
  Dorothy Rivers
- ☐ 1310 TAWNY ARE THE LEAVES
  Wynne May
- ☐ 1325 NO SOONER LOVED
  Pauline Garnar
- ☐ 1332 DON'T WALK ALONE
  Jane Donnelly
- ☐ 1335 THE RED CLIFFS
  Eleanor Farnes
- ☐ 1351 THE GIRL FOR GILLGONG
  Amanda Doyle
- ☐ 1400 THE DISTANT TRAP
  Gloria Bevan
- ☐ 1402 DEAR DOCTOR MARCUS
  Barbara Perkins
- ☐ 1405 THE CURTAIN RISES
  Mary Burchell
- ☐ 1408 THE SILVER FISHES
  Lucy Gillen
- ☐ 1410 NURSE DEBORAH
  Marjorie Norrell
- ☐ 1413 THE FAMILY FACE
  Bethea Creese
- ☐ 1416 SUMMER IN DECEMBER
  Essie Summers
- ☐ 1421 PARISIAN ADVENTURE
  Elizabeth Ashton
- ☐ 1422 THE SOPHISTICATED URCHIN
  Rosalie Henaghan
- ☐ 1423 SULLIVAN'S REEF
  Anne Weale
- ☐ 1424 THE VENGEFUL HEART
  Roberta Leigh

All Books are 50c each. If you cannot obtain these titles at
your local bookseller, use the handy order coupon.

Have You Missed Any of These *Harlequin Romances?*